"I'm always impressed with the quarterly online literary magazine, *Lowestoft Chronicle*—it's filled with intriguing fiction, non-fiction, poetry, and interviews."

—Matthew P. Mayo, Spur Award-winning author of
*Tucker's Reckoning*

"Without a single stinker or filler piece in the bunch, this wonderful 'little' anthology definitely bids well for the strength of work the online magazine version must regularly publish. I was extremely impressed with the variety and quality of the writing. There's something here for everyone to check out between novels while on vacation or holiday, a lunch break, or even while you're waiting to board a plane, train or bus. A solid collection of funny and fine travel-themed stories, poetry, essays and interviews that easily fits in a back pocket or carry-on bag."

— Frank Mundo, *LA Books Examiner*

"*Lowestoft Chronicle* is a superb lit mag. It offers the kind of perceptive, humorous writing that we like here at TCR."

— *The Committee Room*

"There's a lengthy new interview with me at the online magazine the *Lowestoft Chronicle* that I think is one of the best I've done. Lots of information about the early days of my writing career (most of which makes me feel about a thousand years old). *Lowestoft Chronicle* editor Nicholas Litchfield always asks interesting questions and puts together a fine online magazine of fiction, poetry, and writing-related features. Be sure and check out the rest of the contents while you're over there. It takes the reader to a wide variety of literary destinations, and makes even a confirmed hermit like me want to get up and go somewhere. Highly recommended"

—James Reasoner, acclaimed author of the cult classics
*Texas Wind* and *Dust Devils*

"A coruscating cornucopia of humour, drama and big, beautiful adventures. Highly original and entertaining."

—Pam Norfolk, *Lancashire Evening Post*

# SOMEWHERE SOMETIME...

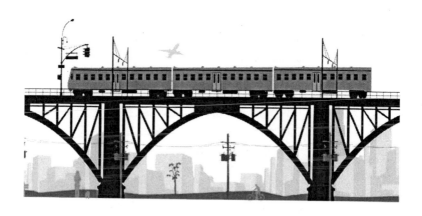

EDITED BY NICHOLAS LITCHFIELD

Lowestoft
Chronicle
Press

SUBMISSIONS

The editors welcome submissions of poetry and prose. For submission
information, please visit our website at www.lowestoftchronicle.com or email:
submissions@lowestoftchronicle.com

Published by Lowestoft Chronicle Press, Cambridge, Massachusetts
www.lowestoftchronicle.com

First Edition: March 2014

Cover design by Tara Litchfield

ISBN 13: 978-0-9825365-7-5
ISBN 10: 0-9825365-7-7

Library of Congress Control Number: 2014932396

Printed in the United States of America

# CONTENTS

"From train stations in Mexico and bus stations in Belize, to marinas in Monaco and *okada* taxi stands in Lagos, our 2014 anthology, *Somewhere, Sometime*, carries a riveting assortment of poetry and prose."

**– editor**

# EDITOR'S NOTE

*Lowestoft Chronicle,* an online literary magazine published quarterly, was founded in 2009, with the first issue launched in March 2010. Although US-based, the name of the magazine was inspired by the English coastal town of Lowestoft, in Suffolk, which once was a regular weekend getaway destination of mine. *Lowestoft Chronicle* carries the distinction of being the city's first and only literary magazine.

Every year, we compile an anthology of the best pieces from the online editions of the magazine, with an eye for travel and adventure. Our fourth anthology is no exception. Among the more outlandish adventures—a young exchange student, five fat German ladies, and a monkey brawl with a stalker after a tense train journey from Besançon, eastern France in "The Exit," by Susan Moorhead. A backpacker, traveling through southern India, is whisked away in a little van on a journey to meet God in John Dennehy's "Forty-five Minutes to God." And in Kim Farleigh's "The Rises and Falls of Svetlana Hiptopski," a short-term head injury causes a successful model to trade her life in Monte Carlo with a smoldering Italian fashion tycoon for an apartment in Bradford with a fat, balding plumber.

Some of the tales are set closer to home but are no less dramatic, such as Chuck Redman's "Christie's Free Way," where a new eight-lane freeway brings a community to a sudden grinding halt, and Tim Conley's "The Bad Father," where a father frantically searches for a unique last-minute birthday present for his ten-year-old daughter.

In some cases, death is the catalyst for travel. In "Flight," by Rob McClure Smith, a woman returns to Glasgow for her father's funeral, while in Nick LaRocca's "Gestures," a reporter travels to Belle Glade, Florida, to cover the murder of a local grocer.

And, sometimes, as in the case of Ed Hamilton's "Rice"—where a tourist in San Francisco, in search of a hamburger, winds up in a trendy vegetarian restaurant—it is less about travel and more about the experience.

Oftentimes, the nonfiction pieces we receive sound so incredible that it's hard to distinguish fact from fiction. My favorites from last year include "The Arsenale," by Nancy Caronia, an affectionate account of a fifty-year-old man living in a cave on the island of Capri, and Michael Solomon's "Hello My Name is Chris—A Confession," where a shrewd screenwriter in New York concocts a travel business to accumulate hundreds of thousands of air miles without having to leave his swivel chair.

Elsewhere, an American woman rides the rails through Mexico in an effort to experience how others live in "Real Life," by in Sue Granzella. On the outskirts of St. Petersburg, backpackers test their luck with cut-price caviar in Yvonne Pesquera's "My Own Special Caviar." And, in "A Dash in Lagos," by Laine Strutton, a foreign student attempts to talk her way out of a shakedown by a street gang in Nigeria.

Poetry renews and deepens the imagination and has always been an integral part of our magazine. Half of our inaugural issue was poetry and it has stayed that way ever since. In this anthology, it accounts for a quarter of the content, and, unlike the fiction and nonfiction, the poems here aren't necessarily about travel. "Time Dilation Case Study: Central America," by Jason Braun, and "French Lesson," by Jackie Strawbridge, are the two exceptions. Otherwise, the poems in *Somewhere, Sometime* exist here because we found them to be so clever and different and memorable that it was difficult to imagine the anthology without them.

Jay Parini, whose poem "Harvest" is included in this collection, is a firm advocate for the vital role poetry plays in society. He argues his case very persuasively in his book, *Why Poetry Matters*. Parini wrote, "I could not live without poetry, which has helped me to live my existence more concretely, more deeply. It has shaped my thinking. It has enlivened my spirit."

In addition to the poetry, short stories, and creative nonfiction, there are a few interviews with some of my favorite writers. The first is with *New York Times* bestselling author James Reasoner, who, during his long and successful writing career, has authored some three hundred novels in a variety of genres, from mystery and Westerns to horror and historical fiction. This interview, a revised and extended version of his second interview for *Lowestoft Chronicle*, covers some of his Western novels, historical fiction, and short stories, as well as his writing process in general.

I've also included my interview with Michael C. Keith, an expert in radio and American culture at Boston College. Author of some two dozen books on electronic media, one of which is the most widely adopted textbook on radio in America, he is also a prolific writer of science fiction stories. Over the years, *Lowestoft Chronicle* has published a number of Keith's short stories, and this anthology includes one of his best ones, "Gertrude's Grave," about a fanatical Gertrude Stein fan who travels to Paris with designs on the perfect cemetery plot.

The last of the interviews is with author Matthew P. Mayo, who won the Western Writers of America's 2013 Spur Award for Best Western Novel. His subsequent novel, *The Hunted*, published the following year is, arguably, even better. My interview with him explores that book, as well as some of his other novels. This anthology also contains a brand new short story by Mayo. "Roadside Attraction" is a humorous 1950s style crime noir featuring a very memorable gorilla.

Somehow, his story feels like the ideal way to close this collection. I hope you will agree.


— Nicholas Litchfield

# THE EXIT

## Susan Moorhead

There was the monkey, and the German women, and the French man who stole my suitcase, and, of course, the bus driver who put the pedal to the metal or I might not even have made the plane. I close my eyes, the day flashes behind my lids, a silent movie, black and white giving way to vivid colors and then fading to a hazy blur. The film's title could be Expat, the story of leaving where I finally fit, home at last among all the other strays and travelers.

If we were going out tonight, Nicole, Zabeth, and me, les trois jolies femmes, our apartment would be a haze of perfume and a clothesline worth of outfits tried on as we decided what to wear, laughing as we shoved each other aside for mirror time. But if they are hitting the town tonight, it is without me. In the course of one day, my year in France has turned into a painted story, a picture book I can look at later in bed. The Sweetgum tree will still guard my window. In bed, in the dark, car lights will sweep past and I will track them across my daisy-strewn wallpaper and feel the height and width of the house, feel the walls around me. Know that terrible quiet of a sleeping house when you can't sleep, electricity in your veins.

Maybe I should start where I ended up, here in hot water, not my usual kind, but in real hot water, sudsy and soothing, bubbles disguising my chin with a fake beard as I sink down in the tub. Below, I can hear the small welcoming party meant for me, just relatives, all of whom assured my mother, as she led me upstairs, that it was perfectly fine that they drove an hour over to greet me two days in a row. I was escorted past them like a celebrity trying to be anonymous.

My mother ran a bubble bath in the tub in the bright yellow hall bathroom rather than in the master bath in my parent's room.

Here, in the top of the stairs bathroom that my sister and I use, I hope no one has to pee. There is no bathroom downstairs. This was not a deliberate act of aggression against the relatives I am sure; it has been a trying day for my mother, and she appears to be running on automatic. Otherwise, there would have been the lecture I expected, how I carelessly mixed up the days and gave them the wrong itinerary, how they waited yesterday for a plane at LaGuardia that never came. How the relatives had to go back to Jersey, how she had to saran wrap the cake, reading the clear message from my aunt's pursed expression, you let that girl run wild and whose fault is that, sending her off at seventeen for a year alone in a strange country.

I called from the airport pay phone in my new fake voice, the one even I know is obnoxious but cannot convince my tongue not to do, so many inflections and pauses and a murmuring of French words. All my native words sound alien to me.

"Come pick me up," I said, listening to my mother's voice rise as she detailed yesterday's wait and worry. How she was absolutely sick with concern and my father was beside himself. I felt a frisson of that worried kind of fear and frustration I have not had to deal with for a year with an ocean between us. "I'm sorry," I said, "I'm here now." I sat on my suitcase smoking the last of my Gauloise, to wait the hour or more it would take for them to drive from Larchmont to the airport, the events of the day running through my mind in an exhausting loop.

We were up before dawn, hung over from the goodbye party the night before, too much cassis and who knows what else, Zabeth rescuing me with her usual thoughtfulness, volunteering to walk me up to the Viotte Station, a relief considering my giant suitcase, the smaller one, my usual big purse, and a large paper shopping bag where I had tossed the overflow. I was low on money from poor planning, so a cab was not an option. There was a light drizzle complicating everything.

Gold and rose colored streaks offered a faint challenge to the gray sky as we walked so quickly up the hill that our breath came out in short bursts, making conversation difficult. When the shopping bag broke, its contents spilling into the gutter, Zabeth and I scrambled to grab handfuls of mementos: drink coasters from a favorite club, postcards of favorite places, a restaurant ashtray I stole, black and white art prints I had found in a thrift store, my watercolors, my poetry books, farewell cards, and silly gifts. We opened up the large suitcase and smashed stuff in where nothing could really fit, the two of us sitting on it to snap it shut. Whatever had rolled down the hill into freshly forming puddles we left, late now, running for the train.

Aching legs, aching arms, aching heart, with no time to ease any of it; purchasing the ticket I had meant to do days before. The train rumbled into life, the porter shouted *Vite, Vite! Hurry, Hurry!* oddly trying to block me from jumping on to the last car, Zabeth throwing the heavy bags on the back metal platform of the caboose as the train lurched forward. Zabeth, face shining up to me like a white lily, my sweet friend from a small country village who found the small city life of Besançon thrilling. Her face was wet with rain and tears and I yelled *Au Revoir*. She is one of the kindest people I have ever met and we will write a few letters and then we will lose touch. *Au Revoir, Au Revoir!*

I forced open the heavy door of the caboose and a stout woman tried to turn me away. Where was I to go? Behind us only the receding railway tracks with Besançon telescoping into an out of focus dot. I ignored her argument by refusing to listen to it. I pushed past her, shoving the larger suitcase with one foot, carrying the smaller one and my purse, when I realized that the car was full of special needs people and their caretakers. There was someone posted at each door and several other caretakers were trying to calm down what seemed like far too many troubled people in one train car. As I made my way through, hands reached out to touch me, bodies pressed against me; excited high-pitched words were tipped into my ears. I was patted like a favorite doll. My small suitcase was grabbed, and I took it back, holding on firmly, which meant I could not fend off the hands. I refused to look upset, years of manners drummed into me, smoothing my face into a polite mask, as I forced myself to stay calm, caretakers and patients careening about me, a babble of chaos, hands stroking and grasping as I pushed my large suitcase with my foot, one short shove at a time, as I guarded my other bag and purse. It was not good, but it was brief. Besides, my mind was still back with Zabeth waving goodbye. There were worse things than being the moment's entertainment.

I was very grateful to note the other cars did not seem to offer the same level of complication, except that they were mostly full. I made my long slog down the aisles, looking into the windowed compartments for an empty seat. In the last car, an older man looked up from his newspaper and with swift, gentlemanly zeal, stood and opened the door for me. While my friends were mostly a few years older than me, he was at least fifty, and I was surprised he invited conversation, complimenting my French. I felt some of the tension of the morning ease off my shoulders.

We talked of the weather, places I had visited. He knew the Food Festival in Dijon; he agreed the flea markets in Paris were *incroyable*, incredible, as well. He told me amusing travel stories about Germany and Italy, and during one animated story he entwined my name, Alison, into his words. I knew I did not tell him my name. I felt the familiar alertness that comes to me in situations that seem to hint at some level of peril stir and waken.

"How do you know my name?" I asked him.

He hesitated, and I sensed the same alertness in him. His eyes flickered up to the luggage rack. "I saw it on your suitcase tags when I helped you lift them to the rack." His voice took on that slightly wounded, how could I have doubted him, tone. I knew this game. I smiled and moved my purse into my lap as if I wanted to rest my arms on it. I leaned my head back against the leather seat; his shoulders relaxed again. I let him talk about things I could ignore and wished I had not shared that I would be changing trains at Alsace-Lorraine. He used my name again, this time with a small smile that held too much familiarity that said he felt I had given him this permission.

"C'est curieux," I said, "it is interesting, but I don't think I have my name written on my luggage tags." I watched his face stiffen. It was time to go.

I stood up, my purse guarding the front of me, but there was a dilemma, the suitcases large and small, on the rack above me. I swung them down one at a time, quickly, aiming towards him, so he could not advance. He was talking loudly, quickly, so many words. He had watched me for months, he knew where I lived, the Cafe Granville and Le Club Cave where I hung out, he named some of my friends, Nils, Zeki, Brielle, Zabeth, Meggie. His face was shining with urgency as he pushed forward to hold the door of our compartment shut. I must understand this, my coming on the train, into his compartment, was a sign, after all this time of admiring me from afar, he now knew we really were meant to be together.

Yeah. He was batshit crazy and, sadly, I was not surprised. I seem to put out some sort of signal, if you have major issues, I'm your girl. At least he did not try to grab me or hurt me; he was still caught up in his delusion that he could persuade me to understand his viewpoint. I was not under any delusion, myself, that there was much chance of help from outside sources. After getting mugged in France with my friend, Brielle, along with more than a handful of interesting and nerve-wracking situations, I had learned to rely on my own resourcefulness. How the police at the station smiled indulgently at Bri when we reported the mugging. How they had asked where we were from—Canada and America—and said to me, you are from New York and yet you complain about our streets? They had no use for the problems of the *étudiants* at the Université de Besançon, especially students like Brielle and me of the foreign variety.

We were standing; he was talking. I was looking up and down the aisle, hoping a porter would come past or a brawny American student. I knew better to hope, but that is my life story, I hope anyway. The train rounded a curve and pulled into the station at Alsace-Lorraine. He had to reach up for his own suitcase on the rack above the seats. I opened the door and shoved my big suitcase into the frame, keeping the door open. I kicked it hard and I jumped after it into the line of people exiting the train. I could hear him call out, *Alison! Alison!* But I knew what he did not, and I made my way left into the press of the special needs group getting off the train in not very orderly rows. Ah, their pet was back. I lost myself in their happy confusion, the matrons shouting and red-faced, and I cut through to the station. My would-be, deranged suitor was nowhere in sight. I bought my ticket for Luxembourg and tried to hang against the walls of the building hoping I would not be seen.

There were a lot of travelers; I heard French and German predominantly, some Italian, but no English. I couldn't help but smile at a group of hefty German women, in their sixties or so, wearing the kind of dresses grandmothers wear, shapeless prints matched with sturdy dark shoes. In their midst, on a leash, was a small monkey dressed in baby girl clothes, and she was clearly the darling of their group. I watched them settle at one of the small cafe tables and enjoy the sun that had broken through the clouds. They fed the monkey a cookie, breaking off little bits at time. The monkey climbed from lap to lap, eliciting coos and laughter. I didn't notice until he was right before me, my train companion, his face set in a determined, stern expression. He was dismayed I did not understand this most important thing about our need to be together. He took my large suitcase in hand, and told me I was coming with him, and started walking away. I had no idea what to do.

I ran after him, and yelled at him to give me back my suitcase; I struggled to remove his hand from the handle, and he grabbed my arm and dragged me along with him. My other suitcase was behind me; my purse fell off my shoulder. I could not get out of his grip. I yelled, and I pummeled him. There was something in his eyes that told me not to stop, even though I was not winning, not even slightly.

And they were upon him. Five fat German ladies pushing him off of me, making him let go of my suitcase, hitting him over and over with their enormous pocketbooks while the monkey screamed excitedly behind them. The man held up his arms to protect his face; he stumbled backwards; they continued their assault. He let me go when the first purse connected with his head. I stood by the monkey, watching my rescuers with awe and wonder. He took off running, his dark suit a little blot down the road under the full glory of the sun. I was shaking, and still trying to process what just happened, when the German ladies gathered me up in their midst. I found myself at their table, my luggage and purse retrieved, drinking a coffee someone bought for me, eating a cookie as the monkey ate hers, her head tilted, looking at me with great curiosity. I didn't know what to say to them besides a simple *danke*, thank you, over and over.

During my train ride to Luxembourg, I stared out the window and thought I should try to work my mind like a camera to remember the green crayoned smear of passing trees, the fleecy sheep in a field gone in a wink. I was too tired and upset from my encounter to think anything beyond that. I didn't even realize that the train was running late, but when I got to Luxembourg, the bus I needed had already left. I got on the next small airport bus, but it was clear to me that I would not get to the airport on time. I would miss my flight and have to figure out what to do, where to stay, with very little money, hardly enough for a sandwich, having bought two train tickets, a bus ticket, and apparently a lot of rounds for my friends the night before. The bus driver was taking a leisurely approach to driving his bus to the airport and did not appear moved by my explanation that I would miss my flight if he did not drive faster. He was not French, but he might as well have been with the slight shrug he gave in response to my concern about time.

It was all suddenly too much for me. I started to babble about the man, the monkey, the women, the rain, my lack of money, my mementos in the gutter, leaving France, which was breaking my heart since I knew I would not be coming back anytime soon. I had an audience of bored and edgy people sitting on the bus, with little to do but watch the passing scenery before they got to the airport, paying rapt attention to me.

*Come on, help her out*, someone said in French. *Yes, she must make her plane*, called out a woman. *You can get her there on time*, added in a third. Everyone was rallying for me on this bus, and the driver looked up and flashed a grin at me. His day had suddenly become interesting. We careened through the streets with our driver being cheered on by his supportive passengers. We made it there in what must have been record time, and everyone cheered. I would have taken their photographs if my camera hadn't been stolen at the Dijon Youth Hostel by a bunch of boys climbing through the window in the middle of the night. But that's another story.

The plane ride was much the same back as it was going over. I was flying Icelandic Air. Once again, during the brief stopover in Iceland, I stared out the airport windows at the smoky mist over the mountains and told myself, someday, I would come back and walk there. I admired expensive sweaters in their duty free shop. I spent my last money on a coffee and a roll.

At LaGuardia, I waited for my parents to arrive. We do not have an easy relationship, and it was probably just as much a relief for them to see me off for a year as it was for me. No. It was better for me, I thought, doing a quick review of my previous 18 years in my head. Still, I missed the late night hot chocolate chats with my Mom, the customs of our home, like big mugs of tea, the stacks of books and magazines, my mother playing piano, even the big tree outside my bedroom window. I waited for them, exhausted and impatient, hoping things would be better now, hoping they could see how I had become a woman of the world in our year apart, sophisticated, perhaps a bit European like my foreign born Father. I had kohl rimmed eyes, and I sensed everyone walking by, and no one was familiar. I wound my long hair up in a twist, paced, wondered what was taking them so long. I prepared something to say to them, something a bit aloof, adult, so they would realize we were on different footing now. Where were they? And then a hand on my shoulder, and I turned, and it was my mother, her face alight with love and happiness. I burst into tears. I was appalled at myself, but I could not stop crying until we were in the car, and, even then, I was snuffling and nodding off, rocked by a depth of exhaustion and emotion I did not understand, still don't understand.

I listen to the hum of my relatives talking downstairs and think I need to get out of this bubble bath soon and free up the bathroom. I hold my breath and close my eyes and slide under the surface, the sounds of the house distorted by the water, and for a moment I am no place at all.

# TIME DILATION CASE STUDY: CENTRAL AMERICA

**Jason Braun**

If you bought a bus ticket to Flores
yesterday, then it does not equal
100 USD today. The man
who sold it to you asks to see the ticket,
smiles, and then asks again.
You think about traveler's checks,
passports, the CIA website stats,
and the number of heads cut off between
Guatemala and here. *The ticket*,
he asks, and you wonder, did I interrupt
something between him and this ticket?
If Nikola Tesla can fall in love with a pigeon,
then this guy, who knows? Minutes before
the bus should depart, he returns the ticket
defaced. Alta Vista Bus Tour
has been crossed out and El Mundo Maya
inked over the top. Your bus isn't coming,
and he smiles as an explanation.
He points to a young woman who takes us
to another bus station. Three hours later
an extended minivan pulls up to thirty-five gringos.
You are the last to board and ride shotgun,
the driver's new co-pilot, he eyes you wildly.
You will wait for yet another
half-hour before this bus moves through
Belize City. The Hopi have no word
for simultaneous, but in Belize they speak
English, Jamaican, and Spanish all

at the same time. You get to Flores
slowly, you buy a hand-carved *tortuga*
because you like the word, and the world
is turtles all the way down.

And the alternate ending haunts:
there's another you, who played
by the AAA rules, didn't give
your ticket to Mr. Shady, and still curbside,
head nodding to the reggae, talking to pigeons
that may or may not have arrived on time.

# FORTY-FIVE MINUTES TO GOD

**John Dennehy**

Halfway through a two-month-long trip backpacking through the south of India, I went to an elephant sanctuary. I was taking pictures when a man casually asked if I would like to meet God.

"How far away is he?" I asked.

"Very close. We have a van and we can take you. Only forty-five minutes." He motioned toward the rest of his party, another Indian man and four Eastern European women.

A curious smile spread across my face as my mind flashed back to my near drowning two days earlier.

"Ok, I'll go," I said shrugging my shoulders and laughing out loud.

The small, white van was from the early 1980s and had three rows of seats. The front and back were benches that could fit three across. The middle bench was not as wide, to give an aisle next to the sliding door, and could only fit two. I sat in the front between Ravi and Mumumbai, the two middle aged Indian men in our group. They wore short-sleeved collared shirts, had the typical dark skin tone of the area and, like almost all Indian men I had met, had thick black mustaches.

When Ravi pressed on the gas and we sped away from the elephants, everyone broke into song. I didn't recognize the language, but everyone knew the words and swayed their heads back and forth in unison—and I had the distinct feeling that I had just joined a cult. I smiled at the improbability of the situation, of how one thing inevitably leads to another.

The four pale-skinned women sat behind us. The oldest in the group seemed to be the one in charge. She was stern and said she was from East Germany—a nation that hadn't existed since the fall of the Soviet Union. She was the only woman the Indian men spoke with. They called her Mom.

All the women wore a thin cloth to cover their heads, but only Mom didn't let any hair spill out over the sides or back. It looked as if she may have actually been bald, but I never asked. No one in the group spoke more than a few words of English, so other than inquiring how much time I should budget for the journey to God, I didn't ask many questions.

Two of the women were young sisters from Russia. They looked like they were close to my own age, somewhere in their mid-twenties. They each wore a long flowing silk dress that covered their entire body, save for their bare feet in sandals. I found the one in pink, with her jet-black hair and light pink lips, rather attractive in that you're-in-a-cult-I'm-in-a-cult-I-wonder-what-else-we-have-in-common sort of way. I smiled at her longer than the rest when we struggled to exchange names and countries of origin. She smiled back, but shrunk her head into her shoulders when we broke eye contact. The fourth woman was from the Ukraine and quiet. She was older than the sisters, but a few years younger than Mom.

The men spoke to each other in an Indian language, probably Malayalam. The women spoke Russian among themselves. I had no idea how they had come together, speeding down the Arabian Sea searching for salvation, but I was interested in finding out.

After an hour, we stopped and piled out of the van, but it was just a Hindu temple we had stopped to look at. The men stayed next to the van and smoked cigarettes. I went inside with the four women. There was a concrete ramp that went around in circles as it slowly climbed upwards—the kind they usually have at stadiums in the United States. Every fifteen or twenty feet there was a small statue tucked into a cut-out in the wall. Men with six arms, elephants on two legs and women sitting, well, Indian style, with their hands clasped together in front of them. Next to each figure was a plaque in Hindi, or some other language I didn't understand. The women walked up to each of the small statues alone and studied them as curious children would. Sometimes, they moved on quickly, and sometimes they moved their lips, as if talking to themselves, and bowed their heads forward. I tried to mimic them, and whispered one-sided conversations to the figurines. I didn't believe I was doing more than talking to carved stone, but I thought I should try and fit in. Growing up in a Catholic family, the ritual reminded me of doing the Stations of the Cross when I was an alter boy a lifetime ago.

Returning to the van, I climbed in the back door and sat in the middle seat next to the quiet Ukrainian woman. The pretty Russian girl moved to the back and sat diagonal from me. She smiled at me again when she sat down.

An hour later, we stopped at another temple. I tried to ask where God was, reminding them that forty-five minutes had long since passed, but it was difficult to communicate and I'm not sure anyone really understood. The only responses I got were, "soon" or "He is close."

I never asked again and debated abandoning the group to continue on my own. I had barely spoken with anyone and didn't know why they had asked me to join, or where we were going, or how it would all end—but part of me reveled in the mystery. By this time, I had decided that the women were kind souls and I felt none of the apprehension or fear one may expect when joining a cult on a whim. I was comfortable and had nothing else to do— plus, there was the cute Russian girl—so I got back in the van and strangely looked forward to the ride ahead.

A few minutes later, we pulled over onto a dusty shoulder next to a roadside teashop. The men got out and sipped chai. The women stayed inside or close to the van and offered me their food. We drank water and ate plums and nuts, sucking mango juice and smiling at each other in silence. When our break ended and the van rolled forward again, I nodded my head and exaggerated a smile to try and tell Mom that I was thankful.

The men seemed as if they were working, hired locals paid to transport the religious pilgrims, and so it became the women that held my greater interest. They each had a tranquility and serenity to them that I had rarely seen before. Whatever it was they were after, part of me wanted what they already had.

We drove for a long time. A few hours, I guess—I don't think any of us had a watch. Finally, another Hindu temple, but this time a well-dressed man standing at the entrance denied us admission. There was a sign in English that read "Only Hindu Allowed." I thought we were Hindu, but I guess the doorman didn't. Mom was upset, but Ravi was able to persuade her to get back in the van without making a scene.

Hinduism holds a large umbrella with many Gods, and while everyone prays to Shiva, Ganesha, and a few other big ones, different Hindus do not all believe in the same deity. There is a lot of overlap, but the religion and specific idols worshiped differ from one person to the next. I had thought Mom and the rest of them just happened to be particularly devout to one of the Gods who also happened to be living. If they weren't Hindu, I don't see why we would have stopped at all those temples, but there was a lot I didn't understand.

When night fell, we went to the house of one of the other members of the sect. The area was extremely rural and heavily forested, and the van slowed to a crawl to allow it to pass over the bumps and drops of the empty dirt roads. As we pulled up to a small, indiscreet house, a middle-aged man and woman greeted us—as if they somehow knew the exact moment we would arrive. The woman had glasses and wore a silk wrap that featured a flower pattern. The man was bare-chested and had a thin, white cloth wrapped around his waist. They didn't wear anything to cover their salt and pepper hair, and both had what looked like orange colored chalk drawn in a messy circle on their foreheads.

Inside, there were two rooms; one had a table and folding chairs, and the other was mostly bare, save for one cushioned chair and scattered boxes. In the corner of the second room was a photograph of an elderly Indian man. Beads were draped on the picture and fresh candles were burning on top of a pile of multicolored wax from the dead candles before them. I wondered if he was God. I didn't get a chance to look around much before I was ushered into what seemed to be the only bedroom in the house. When the couple showed me the bed, I realized they meant for me to sleep there.

"Oh no, I couldn't."

"But we insist; you are our guest."

Or at least that's how I interpreted the hand movements and unrecognizable sounds we threw at each other. I'm not sure where everyone else slept, but I think I had the best spot—and my bed was just a dirty sheet draped over planks of wood.

Staring into the darkness of the unknown house somewhere in rural India, I was happy to be alive. Two nights before, I had gone swimming in the Arabian Sea. It was dark, the water was rough, and a riptide swept me out in to the open water. There were no lights on the shore, and the waves seemed to be crashing into each other rather than toward the land. I didn't know where the beach was, and I didn't think I would make it back. Though at the time I considered myself agnostic, I prayed to God to spare my life. I had the conscious thought that death was approaching—and I trembled before forces far greater than my own understanding.

I woke up to people talking outside at sunrise. We sat in the folding chairs at the table and ate rice, fruits, and nuts before getting back in the van and leaving the couple alone in their house again. No one showered or changed clothes. The only bathroom I ever used was a cluster of trees outside the house, and as far as I know, that's all there was.

We drove and drove, stopping at another temple, then drove some more. For lunch, the men went inside a roadside restaurant. I stayed in the van with the women and ate more mangos, plums, and nuts.

In the afternoon, we stopped at a train station and went inside to look at the schedule. Ravi told me, "God is on a train," before we started driving again. I wasn't sure what was happening, but God was beginning to seem distant, and I was no longer sure we would catch him, even by train. The train station was in Palakkad, the first city we had been in during our thirty some odd hours together. We hit a red light at an intersection downtown, and I decided to make that my end. I grabbed my bag and said "Thank you" slowly and clearly three times, opened the door, and walked away without looking back.

# A CONVERSATION WITH JAMES REASONER

*Lowestoft Chronicle*, **February 2013 & January 2014**

James Reasoner (photography: Livia Reasoner)

For more than twenty-five years, James Reasoner has been spinning tales about the American West. His novels and short stories have garnered praise from *Publishers Weekly*, *Booklist*, the *Library Journal*, and the *Los Angeles Times*, as well as appearing on the *New York Times* and *USA Today* bestseller lists. The novels, *Cossack Three Ponies* and *Under Outlaw Flags*, were nominated for the Spur Award, and *Redemption, Kansas*, the first book in his recent Western series, won the Peacemaker Award. One of the most prolific and in-demand Western writers working today, his latest work is considered some of his best.

In a special interview for *Lowestoft Chronicle*, James Reasoner talks about his writing process—from the idea for a story, to the outline, and from the first sentence, to seeing the finished product on the shelf.

**Lowestoft Chronicle [LC]:** You've said in the past that you get a lot of ideas for novels from history books, which is why you've done many historical novels. In terms of writing a Western, what is your initial process for starting a new novel—an original novel that isn't part of a series (yet) and will have your name on the cover? Does the story shape the characters or the other way around?

**James Reasoner [JR]:** Even though I've always thought of myself as more of a "plot guy" than a "character guy," looking back on it, I see that many of my books started with an interesting character. When I started working on my novella, *Savage Blood*, all I really had in my head was a one-armed bartender, and I worked from there figuring out who he was, what had happened to him, and where he was going in his life. My Judge Earl Stark novels certainly came about because of the character.

Of course, if I'm writing something centered around a particular historical event or setting, I start by asking myself what sort of characters would have been there.

**LC:** You once wrote, "In my novels, characters who weren't even in the outline have shown up and played major roles in the books." How detailed are your outlines before you begin work on a book? How structured are your plots?

**JR:** I've written books from one-paragraph outlines, and I've written books from 60-page outlines . . . and everything in between. I've even written books with no outline, just a general idea. These days my outlines usually run three to six pages, really just a fairly detailed synopsis. I always have the beginning, some of the middle, and the end, although the ending can change along the way. Also, as I'm writing, I have a tendency to make notes in the file itself about things I want to include later on. By the end of the book, I may have a couple of pages of notes like that, tacked on to the end of the text, which then get deleted, of course.

**LC:** You've also said that you don't outline short stories. How would you describe your method for writing a short story?

**JR:** Short stories usually get worked out in my head before I start. If I don't have a pretty clear idea of everything that's going to happen, I sometimes get bogged down and can't finish. I have a number of partially written short stories on my computer. And from time to time, I go back and look at one of them and think, "Oh, of course that's what I need to do!" and then I can finish it.

**LC:** In the case of your *Redemption* series, there's a lot of depth and humanity to many of the characters, particularly Eden and Bill. In fact, the first third of *Redemption, Kansas* (book #1) is largely focused on these two characters and their growing love for each other. Was it always your intention with this series to focus on creating characters that would resonate with the reader or did it just happen that way during the writing?

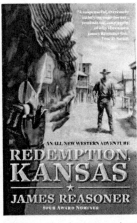

Redemption, Kansas | Berkley Books | 2011

**JR:** I knew the *Redemption* series would run for at least three books, so yes, I wanted characters the readers would like and identify with. Most Western series set in towns go back to *Gunsmoke* for their inspiration, with a strong set of core characters who can interact with each other and the other characters who pass through the books. And with Bill and Eden, I got to write about the sort of characters who really hadn't appeared much in my work, a young couple falling in love and getting married. So in a very basic way, the *Redemption* books are romances . . . with lots of ridin' and shootin', of course.

**LC:** How did this series come about? Had you already started work on the books before the publisher Berkley got involved?

**JR:** The proposal for the book that became *Redemption, Kansas* already existed, so when my agent told me Berkley wanted to see a series idea from me, I pulled it out to see if it would work. It wound up being heavily rewritten, but the basic plot, the town, and the characters of Eden and Bill were already there.

**LC:** The third book in the series, *Redemption: Trackdown*, is one of my favorites of all your books. Somehow, you managed to keep up a fast pace for the entire book! Will there be a fourth installment? It feels like the feud between the Gentrys and Shelton has a twist or two still to come, and I think you put that English gypsy, Gregor, in the book so that he could play a larger part in the next one.

**JR:** My editor, Faith Black, deserves some of the credit for the fast pace, as she made some excellent suggestions about how to structure the book. I'm afraid the *Redemption* series may fall victim to the time crunch that always seems to hover over me. I was indeed setting things up for future books, but there's no time this year to do one and next year is starting to fill up as well. The *Wind River* series may wind up suffering the same fate. I have a stand-alone Western novel I want to write, if I can find the time. I'd like to get at least two new projects with my name on them out this year, more if I can manage it.

**LC:** How would you say your *Longarm* books differ to those of Harry Whittington, Will C. Knott, and Lou Cameron, who also wrote for the series? Did working off Cameron's outlines for the first couple of *Longarm* books shape your writing beyond the *Longarm* series?

**JR:** I think my *Longarm* novels probably have more humor in them than the ones by Whittington and Knott, and many of them have stronger mystery elements than the entries by those two authors. In that respect, my Longarms pretty closely resemble those of Cameron, who was my strongest influence in working on that series. But I think my *Longarms* developed a distinctive style of their own, more influenced by pulps and movies than those of the other authors, and more over-the-top at times as well. By the time I wrote those first two *Longarms* from Cameron outlines, I had already written quite a few novels, so I don't think they had any real influence on my other writing after that.

**LC:** The novella *The Silver Alibi* (published December 2012) is the long-awaited new adventure featuring the wonderful Judge Earl Stark, widely considered one of your best characters. With the exception of the short story "Deadlock" (published August 2002 in the *Guns of the West* anthology) this is the first lengthy Big Earl tale since 1994. Why did you stop writing the series? What made you finally bring the character back? And will there be more Big Earl adventures in the future?

**JR:** There's one other Big Earl story, "'Tis the Season for Justice," in the anthology *Christmas Campfire Companion*, published by Port Yonder Press. I stopped writing the series because Pocket Books didn't offer another contract after the first three novels, but I've always been fond of the character. I can't reprint the first three novels because the deal for them went through Book Creations Inc. (BCI), the book packaging company I worked for at the time, and BCI still controls the rights to those. But the character belongs to me, so I finally decided to bring him back. Back in the nineties, I had a plot worked out for the next novel, if there had been one, and the title was *The Silver Alibi*. I remembered that, although the outline is long since lost, and I have no idea what the plot was for that one. So I wrote a brand-new outline for a short novel called *The Silver Alibi*, and that's the one that was published recently. Projects like this have to be worked in between some of my other commitments, so that's why it's not a full-length novel. However, I do plan to keep spinning yarns featuring Big Earl.

After slowing down in the latter part of last year, I'm back up to my old pace again. Don't know how long it'll last, but I'm determined to get that one more million-word year. After that, who knows? (I seem to say that a lot.) Right now I have four or five books lined up to write in 2015, and if more don't come along I'll just write some of my own. For me, slowing down would be writing three-quarters of a million words. If I only wrote half a million, I might feel like I was retired!

I came close to writing a Big Earl novella toward the end of last year, but I couldn't get the plot to work out and that slowdown I mentioned kept me from ever having the time anyway. But I have the title and part of the plot, and I still plan to get it done sometime this year.

**LC:** Incidentally, did you ever write the story of the talkative little girl named Mockingbird you allude to in *The Diablo Grant*? If not, is there any chance you'll pen the tale?

**JR:** No, I never wrote that one. No plans to, right now, but you never know.

**LC:** While I am a fan of Big Earl, I think many of the smaller characters in the Stark series are also memorable (like the coarse Sheriff Boone Higgins and the ambitious newspaper editor, Matt Curry, from *The Diablo Grant*, and the bellicose court judge, Artemus Buchanan, from *Stark's Justice*, to name a few). A lot of your side characters in the *Stark* series seem ripe for more adventures. Did you ever consider bringing some of them back when you brought back Earl?

**JR:** No, those books are too far back in my writing career, and I like the idea of making the *Stark* books true stand-alones. I sort of miss the days when you could read a series in any order without having to worry about backstory.

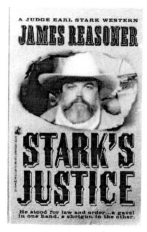

**LC:** I remember you saying that the editors at BCI were pretty hands on. How much control did you have over the finished books? Did they ask for a lot of rewrites and changes? Did the workload ever become a problem for you?

**JR:** The editors at BCI were hands-on when it came to outlines. That's why they liked longer, more detailed outlines, so they would have a good idea of what the book would be like and they could tweak it if necessary at that stage, rather than later on. I had a really good relationship with all of my editors there, and while they usually wanted changes in the outlines, they were open to talking about it. Often, if they felt that something didn't quite work, they would suggest some other way of handling that part of the book, then I would come back with a revision of that, and we just kept it up until we had something that everybody liked. While I wasn't fond of writing long outlines, I have to admit the process worked pretty well most of the time. I don't recall ever having to do any major rewrites on a BCI book. They asked me to once, but I felt like the changes they wanted would be a mistake and was able to convince them I was right on most of the points.

I didn't have any control over the finished books, however. I turned in my manuscripts and never saw the finished product until it went to the publishers. BCI had a "house style," and I'm sure there may have been some editorial rewriting of my books to make them conform to that style, but probably not much. For one thing, I read a bunch of BCI books in various series before I ever wrote for them, so I had a pretty good idea of how they wanted things done. After my first couple of books, my main editor there mentioned a few things I was in the habit of doing that didn't mesh with their style, so after that, I didn't do them anymore. Pretty simple, really. And as time went on and I wrote more and more books for them, they asked for fewer changes and sort of turned me loose to do what I wanted, within reason, of course.

The workload was never a problem as far as I was concerned. At one point, it looked like it might be, which led to me collaborating with Bill Crider on four of the *Cody's Law* novels, but as things worked out, I probably could have done all of them. I would have missed the chance to work with Bill, though, which was a very enjoyable experience, so I'm glad things went the way they did.

LC: During your long and productive career, were you ever in the position of having to work off an outline you thought was lousy or did you always have control over that side? And were there times when you agreed to a book or book series but wished you hadn't?

JR: There have been only a few times when I had to work from someone else's outline: I've talked about the two *Longarms* I wrote from Lou Cameron outlines, and in two or three other cases, I've stepped in at the last minute to write some house-name books where someone else wrote the outlines. A couple of times, I've written books where not only were the outlines done before I was ever involved, but so were the covers. But it's never been a real problem making my manuscripts match up with the cover copy, etc. I've always been able to put my own spin on the stories, so I didn't mind if the outlines weren't exactly what I would have done with the same plot.

Of course, there have been a number of occasions where I've written books from outlines that my wife, Livia, has done, but that's not really the same thing. She knows my strengths and weaknesses and always gives me great stuff to work with.

There have been a few jobs I've taken that I wished I hadn't. Once I was hired to rewrite an unsold manuscript. It was a big romantic suspense/woman in jeopardy novel by an unpublished author who was willing to pay to have the manuscript doctored. That job involved rewrite after rewrite, to the point that I began calling it "the book that wouldn't die." I got paid, but I don't think I ever satisfied the person I was working for, and as far as I know, the book never sold. Another time I was hired to ghost a novel for an author unable to deliver on a contract because of health problems. What I didn't know until after I'd written the entire book was that it was already three years overdue and the publisher didn't really want it anymore. That was one I never got paid for, and that book was never published, either. There have been a few other ghostwriting jobs that didn't go very smoothly, but everything worked out all right in the end.

LC: Last year I read a fantastic book of yours titled *The Wilderness Road*. I'm surprised it isn't one of your better-known books. I remember thinking, halfway through, that there were a lot of good storylines you had to resolve in the last hundred or so pages. Of course, you resolved them all. But it made me wonder how you decide what books will be stand-alones and what ones will become a series. Do you shop a series or does the publisher ask you for one? In the case of HarperCollins, for example, why *Wind River* and not a *Wilderness Road* series?

JR: I'm glad you enjoyed *The Wilderness Road*. I've always liked it and think there's some pretty good writing in it. *Wind River* became a series because Harper wanted a Western series and approached our then-agent to see if any of her clients had something. Livia and

I did a proposal for it immediately and got a six-book contract. When the six books were done, they hadn't sold well enough that Harper wanted more, but they had sold well enough that the editor suggested we do some stand-alones. They just didn't want to commit to another multi-book contract. So we wrote the outline for *The Wilderness Road*, sold it, and it did well enough we then sold *The Hunted* to them. But that was the end of it, and I honestly don't remember if Harper didn't want anything else or if Livia and I were busy with other stuff and just never pursued any more stand-alone deals with them. *The Wilderness Road* has gained a whole new life in our e-book reprint, where it's sold consistently well for a couple of years now and is one of our best-selling titles overall.

**LC:** I've read a number of your *Cobb* short stories, which have a great supernatural quality to them, or hint of the supernatural, at any rate. Over 25 years, you've written only five *Cobb* tales— the first, "Hacendado," dates back to 1988. Considering this character's popularity (several of his adventures have been praised by *Booklist*, *Publishers Weekly*, and the *Library Journal*) why haven't you written more? What are your thoughts on the character, and do you plan to write more *Cobb* stories?

**JR:** The first *Cobb* story I wrote was actually "The Wish Book," which wasn't published until after some of the others were. I really enjoy writing about him, and I've done a story with him for *Western Fictioneers* anthologies each of the past two years, "Rattler" in *The Traditional West*, and "Presents for One and All" in *Six-guns and Slay Bells*. So there's a really good chance he'll show up again, but I sure can't say when. I didn't write more of them in the past because there was really no market for them except when I was asked to contribute to an anthology.

I wrote one *Cobb* story that was never published called "The Smokestack." A pretty oddball story, like the others in the series. But the manuscript was lost in the Big Fire of '08. If I still had it, the story would probably be available as an e-book by now. I remember the plot and could write it again, but I doubt if I ever will.

**LC:** What is your process for determining what the title of a novel/short story will be? Is it an easy decision or a challenge?

**JR:** I'm all over the place on titles. Sometimes they just come to me and that's the first thing I have, and sometimes I struggle all the way through a project to find a good one. And a lot of times, they wind up being changed by editors, anyway. I do a lot of series books where the titles may all be similar, so that gives me a foundation to start with on those books. If I like a title and it winds up not being used, I'm liable to try it again on a different book.

**LC:** How important is the first sentence?

**JR:** One of the first pieces of writing advice I ever read was about the importance of a narrative hook. I like to catch the reader right away and often (but not always) that involves action. If it's not action, I try to come up something that will tell the reader something about the main character right away, something that really catches at least one facet of the character's personality.

**LC:** What stage of writing a novel is most satisfying to you?

**JR:** I'd say starting a novel and finishing one are about equal in satisfaction. I really enjoy both of those things. It's all that stuff in the middle that's hard. I still like the end results, too, and by that I mean seeing the books on the shelves or, in the case of e-books, listed on the various outlets for them.

**LC:** Looking back over your writing career, what have been your highlights, and do you have any regrets?

**JR:** There have been many, many highlights: Opening the box that contained the author copies of my first novel on a sunny October morning in 1980. Being able to make a living as a full-time writer. Having books nominated for various awards and actually winning the Peacemaker Award for *Redemption, Kansas*. Appearing on some bestseller lists (not under my own name yet, but that'll come, one of these days). The most satisfying thing, though, has been being able to spend so much time with my family over the past thirty years, which I wouldn't have been able to do if I'd had a regular job.

As for regrets, I've had an opportunity or two that I didn't take advantage of the way I should have. I was invited to contribute to a series that was very successful for a while. The editor even called me and asked me to send him something. But I had other projects going on, and this was early in my career when I hadn't really learned how to use my time, so I never got around to it. Looking back on it now, the job probably wouldn't have helped my career that much, but I didn't know that at the time. So any regrets I have are minor ones, and they all boil down to feeling like I should have worked harder.

# FLIGHT

## Rob McClure Smith

Getting off the plane, walking in a gray mist to the shuttle stop, the rain didn't surprise me in the least. Glasgow reminiscences are drizzly ones. I felt as if I was imposing memory on the sodden turf, just so I could feel at home in a place I once called home, though it never was. Home is where the heart is, and only the fact that a heart had packed up brought me back.

I chewed the gum the stewardess gave me so my ears wouldn't pop. They give gum if you ask, which is nice, and my ears scream on the descent, which isn't. I nibbled the gum into bits, rolled them into gummy balls on my tongue, and spat them out to see how far I could make them fly, winging them off in a saliva spray. I found it enormously entertaining; partly, because I didn't have anything else to do until the shuttle came, mainly, because I was uproariously drunk. I make a point of getting gloriously sloshed on long flights. If the plane is going up in a fireball, I'm prepared to spontaneously combust in advance. I'm not too big on flying. I've never liked it.

There was one observer of my consummate dissipation, but he was not in a position to comment. Arriving at the shelter, I heard him engaged in a heated discussion. He knew I had heard him. I had that on him. It's amazing how often I find myself sitting beside a man who talks to himself. Then again, I've never found the ones who natter to themselves to be terribly dangerous, contrary to the popular stereotype. It's the men who talk to *me* that are the dangerous ones, the degree of danger in inverse proportion to the innocuousness of the approach.

My father was the first to warn me about strange men.

"Watch oot for bearded weirdos," he told me.

That was right before I left for university. He was talking about sex, though he never mentioned the foul deed, directly. I think he tried to once. We were leaning on a three-wired fence, looking at a cow in a field, I have no idea why, and what I recall, with the detail of acute reminiscence, it was a spectacularly ugly, brown heifer.

A pair of butterflies flew between us. "Look, they're fighting," I said. Not because I was a naive eleven-year-old, although I was, but because I noticed him strangely fixated on the aerial jig of their blue-gold coupling and dreaded what I suspected, with adolescent intuition, would follow.

"Naw," he murmured sepulchrally, "Ah think they ur *making love*."

Fearing this the beginning of something *really* embarrassing, I commenced thrashing dementedly at a clump of dandelions, lopping their heads off with the birch twig he'd cut and stripped for me. Their yellow faces had assumed the sallow complexions of all the boys I knew in primary school.

"Ah guess ye know aw aboot that," my father said, picking seedy white wisps out his hair. "They teach it at the academy ah see."

"Yes."

"Well. . .listen. It's important whit they tell ye, pet." By now, he was bearing down on the wire in a way not to do it any good. "Some day ye'll love a boy, when yir older ah mean, and ye'll want tae marry him."

"Uh-huh."

"And then ah'll huv tae pay fur the fuckin weddin'."

By now the cow was looking at us. Ugliness is relative perhaps. Or maybe she wanted to eat the dandelions. And so there we stood, father and daughter, alone together, stricken with mutual embarrassment: the two of us, something slow happening inside the cold brain of a cow.

But the subject was dropped, at least until his sepulchral profundity about strange men six years later, and we'd never pick that thread up again.

*

The shuttle was late. My uncle picked me up at the depot. He didn't pick me up at the airport out of spite.

"There's something stuck tae yir coat. Looks like chewing gum. How'd ye get bits of gum stuck oan yir coat?"

Driving, he told me how sorry he was and how he'd taken care of everything except "the money side of things." The funeral was the next morning. But he hadn't found the key.

"The key to the house?"

"Naw, lass, tae his strongbox. There's this big metal box. That's where it is. He must've kept the lot in there. Aw his statements and life insurance and stocks and shares and that. Ye widnae ken where it's at, eh?"

The tiny red veins on his face suffused with excitement and his hands shook on the wheel, the contours of his skin wobbling like lemon blancmange. If he thought my father was loaded, he was sadly deluded. I was worried about how I'd pay the funeral expenses. Did they have pauper's graveyards? How did you apply for admission?

"Why didn't you break it open?"

I knew my uncle's curiosity, held in check for so long, would have led to him ransacking the apartment. He hadn't been in there for years. Not since his sister died, a convenient excuse to stay away. He never liked my father. My question was mischievous. My uncle would have had to stop short of trying to break into the personal papers.

"Well, ah tried. It's pretty damn sturdy. Ah couldnae wangle the chisel under the flap and the hammer jist put dents in it. We wur gonnae take it tae a locksmith, but it wis a Sunday and they was aw shut, and ah supposed ye'd know."

Because he was a fundamentally appalling human being, I had a tendency to underestimate my uncle. I forget that the more base an individual's tendencies, the more resourceful his attempts to exercise them. This is why I am taken advantage of so often.

Driving on A-74, wipers sloshing, visibility poor, he grew increasingly apoplectic. It wasn't the weather. He didn't like that he hadn't noticed how drunk I was, or the sloppy, casual way I dress when I travel, or my fast fading accent, or that I was not hitched, or the Anglo-Saxon adjective I inserted before British Airways.

Perhaps it was a glimpse of the father in the child.

*

My father would have approved of the weather. In Glasgow Fairs, we vacationed in Rothesay, which is on the current of the Gulf Stream. Anyway, that's how the locals explain the drooping, sick palms on the shorefront like so many ravaged umbrellas. It always rained on the Glasgow Fair. Always. Not tropical rain. Drops to measure your finger by, thick, viscous rain suspended like treacle icicles from the shelters on the shoreline. I still see my father standing outside, in the torrent, engulfed in surrounding blackness, water dripping rope-like from the thick lenses of his specs. Through the hiss of the rain smashing off the tarmac and above the gale that sighed and rocked against the metal stanchions, he'd shout: "Aye, there's a definite break in the clouds. A big bright bit. Definitely lighter back yonder. Ah can see some blue."

I think he secretly harbored ambitions of being a meteorologist. He had this elaborate conspiracy theory that the national weather forecast was biased, that English weathermen had it raining in Scotland as a propaganda ploy.

"That eegit said it wis gonnae rain the day," he'd scoff, gazing up at a murky stratosphere from the veranda door. "Looks nuthin like it. Ye know why they do this? So English people will think it rains up here aw the time. So they'll no visit. So they can ruin oor economy. Whit ur ye laughing at? Whit's so fuckin funny?"

My uncle now broached the subject of my own limited vocabulary.

"Yiv got a terrible tongue oan ye, hen. Must be a bad place tae live if ye carry oan like that. Aw them blacks carrying guns. Nasty place yon States. Huv ye considered movin' back? D'ye no think yir auld man wid have liked his wee lassie hame wi' him?"

He swiveled and stared at me, shifty as a cobra, but I was never one for guilt.

*

He pulled the Cortina up outside the flats and coughed. It was all very familiar, except for my orphan status. By the steps to the Ex-Serviceman's Club, a little girl in a blue gingham dress leaned over her baby carriage, yelled something, and slapped her doll.

I lifted my suitcase out and staggered with it up the curb. The council had repainted the swing doors a deeper red, a splash of scarlet to pep-up those coming home from work—lipstick on a pig. The stairwell was rimed with dirt, and rows of empty milk bottles lined up against the walls like suspects in an identification parade. A faint odor of urine also, which was new.

I pushed the door shut and snibbed it, for here I would be safe from the small wreckages. The flat was peculiarly comforting, everything as I remembered it: the living room with its bird-in-flight green wallpaper; the mantelpiece, canted slightly, with its brass ornaments; the electric fireplace with its plastic shell of orange coals and rotisserie of fake flames. A brand new TV in the corner. Bad timing. My father would have cracked wise about how that was typical of his luck. I lay down on the grotesque brown suede settee. Cigarette burns etched a constellation of holes in the fabric. He was a forty-a-day man. I'd have to sell it all, every last knick-knack, to lowlife antique dealers, con men and shysters all. So many broken things.

I took off my shoes. I closed my eyes. I was home.

"Did you find it?"

The telephone startled me awake.

"Find what?"

"The key tae the strongbox wumman!"

"No, looked everywhere though," I lied.

"Damnation. Well, it'll turn up."

I hung up and the phone rang again.

"No, still haven't broken into it," I said, wearily.

But it was Stephen, checking in. We had a row the day before. We always fight before either of us leaves for a trip. I'm not sure why that is, but I am sure it's unhealthy. He'd been going on and on like he does about Freud and mourning and melancholia and such and I wasn't listening. Honestly, he has the charisma of Zeppo Marx. And here he was, upbeat and chatty, making an effort. Calling transatlantic, suggesting I look for the key in an old teapot or kettle.

That night, I opened the lid of an old teakettle and, inside, was an ancient leather purse, cracked and scuffed. Inside were two tiny, identical keys. I took the strongbox from a shoebox. My uncle had put it there for safekeeping. What was it with the men in my family, with the kettles and shoeboxes? Did they like to hoard, to bury things, a repressed pirate instinct? I took the rest out—old photographs, driving licenses, pencils and crayons, the ivory set of dominoes, air mail envelopes, the tiny key to the grandmother clock.

I found the letter I expected. A half-page typed breakdown of finances. One handwritten line—"Maggie, if anything should happen. . ." The ellipsis to a building society account number. At the bottom, a plastic envelope, different from the others and, inside, photographs of my parents, an Irish honeymoon, vacations at St. Sirus, Lundin Links, stonewalls and cows, and putting greens, and sand pouring from sandals. And the batch of letters I had written, annotated, plastic strips attached—"Maggie moves house, new address" or "Maggie new man friend." I liked "man friend," an oxymoron describing a cavalcade of oxen and morons.

And yet another photograph: an awkwardly gawky, goofily grinning, grimly bespectacled eleven-year-old, holding her kite the way Cleopatra must have her asp. Me. I remembered the kite. My father used to build kites from bamboo and stretched polythene paper. But this one was a bought kite, plastic and metal with a hawk emblazoned on its surface so that, the further it stretched in the sky, the more it looked like a raptor, set to swoop. We'd climb that hill above the quarry, and I'd attach three reels of twine end-to-end and set the kite out in the sky until it was almost invisible, a distant dot, and there was no tug on the line. Sometimes, I thought I could never bring it back. It took hours to rewind the coil.

I unlocked the veranda and stepped outside, my bare feet chill on the concrete. Three socks slung on a rope washing line. The sky, a blue canal spider-webbed by vapor trails.

I used to wonder if the kite was so high that a plane might catch the rope and pull me in to the sky behind it. It scared me, but I felt it would be the most wonderful thing, too. It's such an exhilarating thought: to be pulled into the sky and trail behind a plane forever.

I once asked him if it could happen.

"Ah don't think so. It's no that high. Once it gits a certain height it stops goin' up and goes oot instead. Planes are way higher. Mibbe a really tiny plane could snag it. But it wid take a big jet tae pull ye intae the sky. The rope wid snap anyway afore ye left yir feet."

"Oh." I was so disappointed. I had set my heart on flying.

"Whit ye need tae be careful oaf is the power lines. If the twine touches the cable we wid be electrocuted. There wid be a big flash and jist black grass where yir standin. Ye widnae like that, wid ye?"

I thought for a moment. "No."

"And yir daddy widnae like it neither. Whit wid he do with himself then? Whit wid he do if his wee lassie went away frae him?"

I remember telling him that I didn't know.

# A BOOK ENTITLED *THE HISTORY OF FURNITURE*

**Andrew House**

Option One:
> The casual reader devours words
> like snicker doodles laced with
> aphorisms. If the dentist's office
> were particularly molassy,
> we'd read a catalog of nose hair
> trimmers just to stifle our
> jumpiness.

Option Two:
> In a lightly mildewed basement
> exists a sweat-stained connoisseur
> of tuffets and fauteuils. His magnum
> opus, an epoch-spanning epic of
> armoires and ottomans, rests
> in my hands like a lost book
> of God.

Option Three:
> The pinball machine of human
> knowledge runs on the same principle
> as the Feeding of the 5,000. If we don't
> snatch the triple multi-ball, that rolling silver
> heart will slide past our hands. A low note
> will play, and we'll press our rotted faces
> to the glass.

# REAL LIFE

**Sue Granzella**

My left butt cheek was the only part of me that could fall asleep on the cold cement floor of the Guadalajara train station. I sighed, scooting a few inches closer to the back that was pressed against my own. I'd wanted to see as much of "real life" as I could during my last week in Mexico. Leaning butt-cheek-to-cheek at three in the morning as part of a long chain of strangers, with the rain streaming on us through the badly leaking roof, I was acutely aware of how real it felt. Rubbing my bleary eyes, I yawned.

Just a week earlier, in July of 1989, my traveling buddies had flown back to California, and I'd headed to the Uruapan train station to buy a second-class ticket to Morelia, Michoacán. My upbringing in Napa, California, had been frugal, but despite my learned thriftiness and simple lifestyle, I did have enough money at age thirty to pay the very low cost of a first-class Mexican train ticket. I didn't want to ride that train, though. Ever since I'd been a Catholic elementary school kid and heard visiting missionary priests describe how people (especially impoverished people) around the world lived, I'd wanted to understand better the struggles that other people face. My parents each did volunteer work around town, both with elderly people and with low-income people, and I grew up with the knowledge that life was a lot bigger than what I experienced. I appreciated my own circumstances, but my desire to feel more connected to others outside my own sphere only increased as I got older. I felt like my life would be richer, more filled out, more complete if I had experiences that would show me more about how others lived. The grittier aspects of life for those who didn't have it easy—that's what I thought of as *real* life.

So as a young adult, I found jobs and volunteer positions that enabled me to brush up against some of the "real life" I craved. In my twenties, I worked in Oakland with immigrants and refugees, and this further opened my eyes to a world very different from the comfortable one I'd known growing up. I began longing to understand more of what these people had left behind in their home countries. So that summer, when I was thirty, I had chosen Mexico for my vacation, pledging to visit the villages from which my immigrant friends had come, to see some of their "real life."

At the train station, I sidestepped some spindly-legged five-year-olds who were selling pieces of *chicle* (gum) at ten for a penny, and clambered up the metal steps of my car. A first-class Mexican train had cushioned seats, but in the second-class train there were rows of worn wooden benches instead. The car had an almost festive feel, though. Children outnumbered adults by about three to one, and most of them chattered noisily. Women in faded cotton flowered dresses spread out picnic lunches, busily handing *tortas* to men in leather boots caked with dried mud. A skinny ten-year-old with a cardboard box strapped to his shoulders snaked in and out among the travelers, peddling his baggies of juicy sliced watermelon and mango. Since my *Lonely Planet* book had shouted at me in bold print that underno circumstances was I ever to succumb to the temptations of fruit from street vendors, I reluctantly turned away from him.

As we lurched into the start of our journey, a fluttering collection of little white flags hanging from the windows of our car cheerily waved good-bye to the station. Not until we had built up some speed, and the breeze was ruffling my hair, did I realize the little flags were cloth diapers that resourceful mothers had hung out to dry.

As I scanned the car for a seat, a round woman with a sun-browned face and smiling eyes waved me over to sit next to her and her husband. He was as thin and angular as she was round, his heavy leather belt cinched in tight. Within ten minutes, Lupe was plying me with bananas and hunks of coarse brown bread. Within twenty minutes, she was eagerly dictating directions to their home in the countryside. I was glad my Spanish was good enough to catch "*after the long fence*" and "*past the second road in the field.*" I assured her that I would try to come in a few days for a visit.

The rest of the day's journey passed in similarly hospitable fashion. As the crowded and dilapidated train creaked and groaned past rivers and valleys, the occupants of my car called out one to another, strangers-turned-friends, ooh-ing and aah-ing in appreciation of the lovely scenery. Women who I suspected were younger than they looked called out, "*This side!*" when the sights on the right or the left were especially striking. Teenage boys made space for grown men to glimpse the world out the window. It may have been just real life to them but, to me, the easy friendliness of the people was how I envisioned heaven. I found myself feeling proud of the people in my car. Second-class? I think not!

True to my word, after visiting Morelia and Patzcuaro, I boarded a bus to visit Lupe, my friend from the train. Following her directions, I hopped off the bus where two dirt paths crossed the road, just past a tiny market. The bus lumbered off through the fields and left me coated in a cloud of dust, trudging past the long fence toward Lupe's house. As I walked, I wondered about the wisdom of what I was doing. Here I was planning to stay overnight with a family I'd chatted with—in my less-than-sparkling Spanish—for two hours. Had I even told them my name?

Over the next twenty-four hours, I was enfolded into the warmth of their family. Bouncing along in a small wooden cart pulled by a donkey, I was given a tour of the dusty roads of their settlement. The eldest daughter taught me how to wash my shirt down at the creek without ripping the fabric on rocks. We snacked on *nopales*, slivers of cactus pads swimming in tangy limejuice. Lupe kept her promise to teach me how to make authentic *chiles rellenos* lightly fried in a golden batter.

After dinner, we sat outside in the quiet of the black night. We sipped hot chocolate made from warm milk that had sat on the stove all day, after Lupe had bought it fresh that morning from a man down the road who owned a cow. Technically, "we" didn't sip the drink; I was terrified of its unpasteurized tastiness. Which would be worse: to spurn the beverage and offend my hosts or to drink it and possibly contract some horrifying gastro-intestinal disorder? I could see the writer of my *Lonely Planet* shaking his head in disgust as I chose the indecisive middle ground—touching it to my lips again and again, but actually ingesting only a few drops. If Lupe noticed the unchanging level of my chocolate, she never said a word.

I'll never know just why Lupe embraced me so fully into her real-life world that I'd stumbled upon. I only know that her graciousness stayed with me long after she waved good-bye from that dirt path under the next morning's hot sun.

*

The long bus ride from their field to the Guadalajara train station took until midnight, the second half through a heavy summer rain. My trip was nearly over; I would hop on a train the next morning and ride it three days to the California border. Despite the late hour, I'd decided to stop and buy my ticket right then, rather than wait in a morning line. Grabbing my daypack, I ran through the pouring rain, from the bus to the station entrance, and yanked open the heavy door.

I froze. A sea of humanity was sprawled all over the cement floor, except where the sieve of a roof was gushing too much rain. Babies slept in mothers' arms and wizened old men leaned against stone columns. I asked someone what so many people were doing there at that hour and he informed me that they needed train tickets, which wouldn't go on sale until six a.m. I felt betrayed; *Lonely Planet* had not prepared me for this.

Waving *adios* to my hope of a good night's sleep before the morning train, I found the end of the snaky line and claimed my spot of cement. Then I learned a bit about my neighbors for the night. The stocky fortyish man with the pointy cowboy boots was heading north to look for work with his cousin. The old woman, with few teeth and a deeply creased face, was going to Arizona to see her son. Wrapped in a black shawl, she explained that she had financed her trip by selling crocheted doilies, two for roughly a quarter.

Then there was Pedro, a skinny teenager heading for California.

His legs were impossibly long and his jacket sleeves five inches too short, as if he had grown into his manhood too quickly. His serious, take-charge energy and penetrating gaze seemed older than seventeen. I'd never known a seventeen-year-old driven enough to set out alone for a new country. Was he the eldest, determined to provide for his family? I mentally filled in the blanks and suspected that the quiet confidence he exuded was warranted. I got the feeling he had lived much in his brief life. When he spoke, I heard an adult.

He explained to me that Mexico's recent election had spawned civil unrest, prompting a flood of people northward; this scene at the station was definitely not the norm. Pedro told me there were no flights north out of Guadalajara for three days, and every bus north was sold out for a week. Even train tickets were limited, and as I looked at the number of people in that cavernous hall, it began to dawn on me that I might end up stuck in Guadalajara, unable to get home.

My back ached as the night wore on. Mine, apparently, wasn't the only one; a bunch of us paired off, for a while leaning back-to-back against each other. My partner was the doily lady. I could feel her bony spine against mine; I hoped I was providing her some warmth. Although it was terribly uncomfortable, I secretly loved the whole adventure in the station. It definitely counted as real life. Back home, I wouldn't have ever had to sleep on the floor of a train station. I could have borrowed a friend's car, checked a college bulletin board for ride-shares, or just slept on a friend's couch until tickets opened up. I had options; my days were filled with choice, not necessity. I looked around at all these people and knew that my life had to be more comfortable than that of every single one of them. I felt guilty knowing that, but a little less guilty being a little more aware of what people went through without the luxuries that were part of my daily existence. I could never *know* what it was like to be an old woman on a wet cement floor, feeling lucky to have sold enough twelve-cent doilies to have a chance to buy a train ticket. Probably the closest I could get to understanding even a hint of her life was to sleep next to her on the cement floor.

So I was glad to be doing that. It made me feel a little more alive, more whole.

The pounding rain and the murmur of all the voices must have finally lulled me to sleep. When I eventually awoke, I was startled to find myself lying flat on the floor. Pedro was squatting in front of me.

"*Get your money out,*" he directed. The groggy queue was now shuffling toward two ticket windows, under the watchful eye of a guard with a rifle slung across his chest. My sleepy station-mates didn't scare me, but this guy with the big gun gave me the creeps.

An hour became two as we inched closer to the windows. Pedro and another man kept moseying up front to see how many tickets remained; the number they reported back was shrinking. Finally, it was Pedro's turn. After securing his ticket, he turned to me, several spaces behind.

"*Give me your money now!*" he hissed. It wasn't a request; it was an order. I didn't question him. We had talked for hours and slept alongside each other, and something in me knew I could trust him. So I, a thirty-year-old woman, instinctively responded to his seventeen-year-old Mexican savvy. I immediately handed over my cash.

He turned back to the ticket agent, and then came back to me. Quickly, he told me that the train had sold out, and that my ticket had been the second-to-last one sold. He handed me my change and my ticket, and as I looked around in confusion to see if the doily lady had made it, I caught his last words to me: "*We'll have to run!*"

So I ran. I followed Pedro's lead, and as if in the final scene of a cheesy movie, we sprinted through the doorway, toward the last car of the train that was beginning to lurch and creak, already inching its way out of the station.

\*

That trip, more than twenty years ago, wasn't a luxurious vacation. There were long, sweltering bus rides, violent bouts of illness, and nights with creatures crawling over me in the uneasy darkness of dive hotels. But along the way, while sleeping and itching and trudging and sweating through the "real life" I had gone looking for, I was generously received into it, as part of a community. The circumstances I placed myself in were sometimes physically uncomfortable, but those weeks in Mexico left an impression on me, which has lasted much longer than has the memory of any bodily discomfort. With the people of the second-class train car, with Lupe's family, and with my bedfellows on the rainy station floor, I experienced a depth of acceptance, warmth, and welcome that has never left me in the years since. It is that warmth I now remember most from that trip, though I couldn't know back then how tenderly I'd always treasure its memory.

The end came so suddenly that I didn't feel badly until later that day, when I thought about all the people who hadn't made it onto the train. It was all too abrupt and unexpected. All I knew in that last instant was that I didn't have time to think, and that if I wanted to get home, I'd have to run. And so I did, my grubby orange daypack bouncing awkwardly off one shoulder. I jumped for the step of the last car, caught the railing with my free hand, and was on my way north.

# CHRISTIE'S FREE WAY

**Chuck Redman**

Christie was already up and steadily stirring her pale lumpy oat bran over a low flame when Flannery began to bark and a deep rumbling growled up from the cedar floorboards. She had started her day early to allow plenty of time to walk her ancient Schwinn down the dirt road to town and to get the front tire repaired before her Bollywood Dancing class at the community college.

Such barking didn't alarm Christie, since Flannery barked at pretty nearly everything bigger than a child that happened to pass within twenty yards of the old house. But what could cause such an ominous rumbling under her brown-stockinged feet? A low-flying jet airplane, she supposed.

Suddenly, the whole house shook, rattling windows, dishes, and Christie's partial upper plate. Even the goldfish bowl shook and sloshed, which caused a frenzied fluttering about by Agatha and Joyce Carol, who then peered out at Christie with big, panicky eyes and fibrillating fish lips. Flannery's bark turned furious—the way she barked at motorcycles and leaf blowers—and she scratched at the front door. The wooden spoon in Christie's hand fell into the steaming pot of mush.

If we're having an earthquake, she tried to calmly tell herself, I hope it's not quite as bad as the last one. Which was 43 years ago, damaged the old Courthouse and some of the town's best Victorians. The sun is out so it's not a twister, thank God. But earthquakes stop: this tremor didn't. While Flannery scratched and whined, Christie nudged her back from the front door and steadied herself as she slipped her moccasins on. Then she squeezed out onto the porch and shut the door.

Where there should have been, on this dewy April morning, nothing but green grassy fields on the outskirts of town, there were now giant bulldozers and steam shovels lined up for hundreds of yards on either side of her small frame house. Voraciously gulping and chomping huge swallows of grass and ground. Literally, making the earth move.

Nobody heard or noticed Christie, so intent were they to dig and dig, as she padded cautiously out into her front yard, hands up and out to balance herself. Physically and emotionally. They were so intent that the men and machines on the north side didn't even seem to notice there were men and machines on the south side. Or conversely. The equipment on the north side all said Beckerwart Construction. Which jingled a little bell in Christie's throbbing head. Wasn't Beckerwart the maiden name of Congressman O'Donnel's new wife? Moreover, Christie saw that the machines on the south side were from TJN International, which was curious because those are the same initials as Senator Thomas J. (for Jefferson) Nesbitt.

Christie flapped her arms and yelled at the steely-eyed earthmovers, but Christie flapping and yelling is not the most eye-catching of human behavior, because Christie is not a large article and demureness was sewn into her fiber like embroidery in a fine linen handkerchief. Thus, Christie wasted her efforts upon unmindful machinery and was herself unmindful of a simultaneous development: In-between the two long lines of ravenous godzillas, just beyond her front yard to the west, began to grow a mound of dirt fresh from the violent digging. Likewise, behind Christie's house, just past her backyard, another mound started to rise up between the giant apparatus. When she finally gave up waving at the beasts and looked up and down her property, she realized a very succinct fact.

Well, I'll be hog-tied, exclaimed Christie to herself: With huge unstoppable machines on either side, and rising mountains of dirt to the front and to the rear, she was trapped!

She ran inside and switched on the news radio station. "...the five-term senator stated in no uncertain terms that, unless the other party was willing to compromise, there would be no budget and the government would have to shut down at 12:00 a.m on

Friday. We'll keep you updated here at news central with hourly reports straight from the capital...KOPA local news time 7:08. Construction began today on new Highway 117, the recently-approved eight-lane freeway which will connect Little Grove with suburban Centralburg. With round-the-clock construction, officials estimate rapid completion of the project, which is expected to bring much-needed economic growth to the Little Grove area ..."

The physical and the emotional conspired to make this a very wobbly and jarring moment for Christie. Although slumping was not normally part of her vocabulary, she might briefly be forgiven for doing just that. Into her nicely-lacquered kitchen chair, where it became woefully clear that Christie was no longer listening. And had started in worrying—big time—about a million desperate scenarios orbiting her head and about one friend who licked her hand and understood.

Well, as these things usually go, the bulldozers and steam shovels soon gave way to giant graders, pavers, colossal cranes, and cement mixers by the dozens. Dirt trenches became concrete roadways before Christie's searching eyes. The mounds of dirt to the front and the rear were reincarnated as freeway overpasses. Christie's house now sat smack dab in the middle of an eight-lane freeway. And the moment that construction was completed, lines of impatiently-waiting cars and trucks poured onto the freeway like red army ants onto a sleeping fawn.

"Felice, please tell me you made some headway," Christie pleaded breathlessly when her friend, who was a certified paralegal, finally got back to her.

"I wish I could, dear," began Felice in a voice that did nothing to lift Christie's sunken spirits. "First, I went to City Hall. But they told me they don't have jurisdiction because the County has control and maintenance of all highway corridors, including thirty feet on either side of the highway. So I went to the County."

Christie's eyebrows were close-knitted and wary and, holding the telephone tight with both hands, her mouth hung open. She said nothing while Felice's voice rambled on through the wires.

"The County said they can't do anything, Christie, because the highway itself is a State highway and they would need authorization from the State to access the median strip."

"Can't we get authorization from the State?" implored Christie, with deep lines squeezed into her forehead.

"Well. I wrote and I called. The State Department of Highways politely told me that they are not in a position to help us. It seems the State and the County don't get along. They haven't cooperated with each other in years."

"Oh for Pete's sake, Felice! That's not funny." Christie had been doing some deep breathing to try and relax. It wasn't working. So she closed her eyes, shook her head, and mouthed a string of angry, awful words she would never have uttered aloud. That helped a little. Inquiring bleakly if there were any options left, she sat down and rested her elbow on the kitchen table to try and keep the receiver from shaking against her ear.

"Well, all I could think to do was call the Feds, Christie."

"Oh, the Feds."

"The Federal government. You know."

"I know who the Feds are."

"Well—they listened and were sympathetic, but—they have no money left after giving the State the ten billion dollars that it cost to build the freeway. Are you there, Christie? I'm so sorry."

"I guess that's it, then. I might as well be in prison, right, like some, some perpetrator! For fifteen years to life."

Felice had to agree with Christie that yes, quite frankly, she was between a rock and a hard place. And she, Felice, was sorry and didn't know what else to say. Unlike the booming roar from the 117, there was a perfect silence on the other end of the telephone line.

Mornings, as April deepened into May, found Christie stopping, now and then, during her daily routine, and gazing out her bedroom window at the steady stream of traffic heading westbound toward busy Centralburg and its suburbs. Or, warm afternoons in her backyard vegetable patch, she'd often pause to contemplate the cars, trucks, busses, so near she almost felt them graze her copper cheeks, whipping eastward into downtown Little Grove.

Where exactly, she wondered, are they all going in such a hurry? What plans do they have, what are they thinking and feeling as they rocket along? Where is Virginia Leiber heading in her blue Dodge pickup? Probably just needs another bushel of seed corn for her silty acreage over by the river. Where did Candace Crowley get money for a new sports car? Is that Gavin Waller driving his mom's Buick? When did he finally get his license, and why isn't that boy in school right now? Her head pounded with the dizziness of all these comings and goings.

With what little vista was left unobscured, Christie's anxious eyes would search the distant fields, woods, roads, rooftops, where she had loved to wander, catch a matinee, a concert in the park, see the children playing. But, and this should come as no surprise, if there's one thing that Christie wasn't, it was a complainer.

She would have preferred playing canasta with her cronies at the Little Grove community center. But Christie was a good sport and counted herself fortunate that she could now play the license plate game until the cows came home.

She would have preferred doing her regular Monday volunteering at the Boys & Girls Club, showing kids how to make art out of odds and ends. But now she found fulfillment making little chew toys for Flannery out of empty toilet paper rolls.

Every evening, Christie sat on her front porch, humming softly and just slightly sharp, and watched the sun dipping down behind the stately overpass. Flannery dozed nearby, but even if alert, would not have heard her mistress' humming over the din of the late rush hour traffic. The dying sun smeared the western horizon with brilliant blood orange juice, thanks to layers of emissions that the freeway had bestowed upon Little Grove.

Christie sat watching until all she could see were two skinny Christmas trees, a twinkling red one on the right and a blinding white one on the left. She would have preferred, later, in the semi-darkness of her bedroom, being lulled to sleep by gentle crickets and frogs, as before. But she accepted philosophically the perpetual rumble of revving engines as a substitute lullaby, on these nights of long uncertainty.

Christie was no complainer, and yet— she and Flannery had needs.

"Bless you, Stuaaaaaart!" called Christie as she heaved her bag of accumulated garbage over the center divider and into the open cargo door of Stuart's large van. It was a Wednesday, noon, the time when Christie's friend, who was a retired shoe distributor, would make his weekly drive-by, going east at about 35, which was as slow as he dared in the fast lane. For ballast, she tied her finished library book to the garbage. Today, it was *Atlas Shrugged*.

At 3:00 p.m. Stuart came along westbound and tossed her two or three bags of groceries, dog food, and supplies. He also tossed her *Invisible Man* from the library.

"Thanks! See you next . . . Hey, you're losing your bumperrrrrrrr!" yelled Christie, horrified, to the diminishing rear end of Stuart's rust-coated van.

It was lunchtime and Christie was toasting a Swiss cheese on rye and deciding whether to tune in to NPR or *Democracy Now*. She turned the volume up and wondered if the traffic noise was increasing or her hearing declining. Her hearing was suddenly vindicated when a terrible crash reached her ears. She ran outside to see. It was a bad one. In the westbound number 3 lane. A three or four car pile-up. She didn't stop to watch, but ran back inside and called 9-1-1. The 9-1-1 operator didn't believe Christie when she said she lived in the middle of the freeway. She hung up on Christie, threatening to report her for making crank 9-1-1 calls. Hurt and disillusioned, Christie went back outside and was relieved, in part, to see that someone else had called in the accident and paramedics were on the scene.

But she was particularly chagrined to see that, even in the presence of this dreadful reminder that freeways are hazardous, the cars in the two fast lanes were driving just as wildly and heedlessly as ever. Drivers were making indignant gestures at one another and even at the paramedics. One car in the number 1 lane just swerved and cut off a car in the number 2 lane, almost causing another serious accident. Behind the wheel of the car that angrily swerved, Christie thought she recognized Doris Carpenter, one of the nicest ladies in town and one of the most dedicated volunteers at the Little Grove Hospice. It took several moments for all this implausibility to sift and settle into Christie's troubled mind.

Two weeks later, Christie was in her garden, trying to save the few vegetables that hadn't succumbed to exhaust fumes, when they came and put up a sign on the far side of the 117 West. She could just barely make out the words on the sign. She didn't know who Gilbert M. Rademacher was, but now there was a Memorial Highway in his name.

Its solstice having come and gone, June was winding down, and Christie was as aware of that cosmic circumstance as anyone in the tri-county area. She was, in fact, lost in sobering reflection one morning as she picked up freeway litter from her otherwise cozy backyard. As if some unseen hand reached and tapped her on the shoulder, all at once something had changed. It was the air. Or something traveling on the air.

There was a strange stillness. A new noise or—a different noise. Flannery whined, the way she did when she wanted exercise.

"OK, my love. Let's walk." Christie rested her little hand on the big dog's neck, and the two began circling the house. The fact that the eastbound 117 was utterly jammed with vehicles and nothing, not a single car or truck, was moving, didn't register in Christie's consciousness. Not until they got to the westbound side, and the realization hit her: this freeway is full. This freeway is so full that there's nowhere for anyone to go. There's nothing moving for miles, east or west. This freeway is a parking lot.

Christie thought about that for a minute, and then she walked Flannery around the house two more times. She stopped and listened. Still, no movement. She saw a sea of motor vehicles, engines running, drivers honking, swearing. Perspiring, thumping their steering wheels, craning their necks to see what was the problem. Flannery whined and pulled at Christie's sleeve. Christie stood watching for more than a minute. Then she gave the dog a pat on the head, turned, and went inside her house.

When she came out, three minutes later, she held the ottoman from her den. And upon it, her sketchpad, her charcoals, and

Flannery's favorite Frisbee. The ottoman, she placed next to the center divider. And before she knew it, Christie and a barking Flannery were over the divider and making their way through a labyrinth of idling motors and stunned motorists.

People stared. People got drop-jawed and looked around at each other. Christie crossed the westbound 117 and chased her ebullient pooch up the on-ramp and out to the country roads and fields just beyond. The freeway remained like two shuddering, dying snakes.

Sarah Garfield, a June graduate of Centralburg State, was the first one to turn her engine off and get out of her car. She looked around, dazed almost, at her fellow commuters. Then she stiffly wound her way between cars in the direction that Christie had vanished. George and Jerry Moreaux, the vertical blinds sales reps, sheepishly shut down their van, locked it, and hustled off the freeway. A trickle turned into a torrent as more and more frazzled motorists abandoned the westbound freeway. The eastbound travelers soon took their cue and were striding toward the nearest ramp in droves.

The sun climbed high and the hot summer wind dusted the now-silent concrete river, strewn with ten thousand empty machines, like rotting fish in a dried-up creek. And the wind whistled a tune and amused herself. Whispering "freedom" to all her friends who listen best when there's nothing to hear.

# HARVEST

**Jay Parini**

Already in the dark outbuildings
sharpen at the edges
as the dawn anticipates their lines.
The field is smooth now
like the stubble of a young man's beard.
The hay is bundled in the barn at last,
while overhead, above the well-scraped earth:
the razzle-dazzle heaven's spray of stars,
a gloating moon.

One lonely boy looks at that moon,
His rough hands hurting
as he locks the door, dreaming of cities.
He asserts a lame, lop-side smile.
The future he imagines
lies elsewhere, a penthouse paradise
where all the stars spread out beneath him
in the easy pickings of the lamp-lit streets.

# HELLO MY NAME IS CHRIS—A CONFESSION

**Michael Solomon**

Webster's Dictionary defines the word "scam" as "a fraudulent or deceptive act or operation, such as an insurance scam." Conversely, the word "legal" is defined as "conforming to or permitted by law or established rules."

Unfortunately, there is no definition listed for "legal scam," but I know such a thing exists because, for two years, I was the proprietor of one, though like a Mafioso who tells people he's in import/export, I didn't openly claim to be involved in a scam. There is something unseemly about fraud, even the legal type that I did. Whenever I was asked, I'd say I was in the travel business, which was technically true. I sold plane tickets. I just didn't sell them for the same reasons other people did.

Had I started my business anywhere but Manhattan, I suppose I would have had my humble beginnings in a garage, à la Steve Jobs. But not only didn't I have a garage, I barely had an apartment. I was sharing a loft downtown with three roommates: a straight painter, a gay publicist, and a bisexual waitress. Thus, I decided to set up shop in the much tinier apartment of my best friend, who had a day job that kept him out during business hours. He lived in a two hundred square foot studio, which is similar to a garage, only smaller. You could find yourself in his living room, kitchen, and bedroom, all at the same time. Stretch out a leg and you entered the bathroom.

I began by having my own phone line installed, which was traditionally how one started a business in America. Even if no one called you, you could always amuse yourself with the thought that the great change you'd been waiting for your whole life was just a phone call away. I always tempered this hopefulness by remembering the old joke that, when my ship finally came in, I'd probably be at the airport. And in a sense, I was.

My plan was to capitalize on the new frequent flyer programs begun by all the airlines. While frequent business travelers—the *true* frequent fliers—were accumulating hundreds of thousands of mileage credits, the rest of the population either wasn't flying enough to ever get any awards, or they used several different airlines and never accumulated much mileage on any particular one. My idea—or rather, my mother's idea—was to accumulate as much mileage as I could, without actually having to fly on an airplane. I would simply exploit a flaw in airline security that, in retrospect, smacks of a truly worry-free era.

My mother owned her own travel agency in California. I was a struggling screenwriter in New York. Mom was always looking for ways to keep me from starving myself to death through chronic unemployment. When I set up shop in 1984, airport security in the United States was far less stringent than elsewhere. You could fly domestically without having to show any identification. All you needed was a ticket. I took out an advertisement in *The Village Voice*, in the travel section, that read: "Fly to Los Angeles or San Francisco, only $49 round trip."

Underneath the ad was my company's name and telephone number, both of which I'll reveal once the statute of limitations expires for businesses that aren't-quite-illegal-but-I'm-taking-no-chances-especially-since-my-mother-is-involved.

At the time, the airlines were engaged in such fierce competition that they offered coast-to-coast flights for only $99 roundtrip, a fare almost anyone could afford. I was selling the same tickets for only half as much, and I got hundreds of phone calls right from the start, which usually went something like this:

"How come your prices are so cheap? Are you for real?"

One way you can tell a New Yorker is suspicious is when they don't bother with "hello." They just jump right into their skepticism.

"I'm not really cheaper than anyone else," I'd say. "The deal is you buy your ticket from me for the lowest available fare, currently $99, but when you come back from your trip, if you bring me your boarding pass, I'll pay you $50 for it."

"What's in it for you?"

"I get your mileage. All you have to do is let me put whatever name I want on your ticket. Since no one asks for ID at the airport, it doesn't matter under what name you fly. The boarding pass is proof for me that you took the flight."

"Sounds illegal."

"I know. But it's not. There's no law that says you have to have your real name on your ticket for a domestic flight. The name I'm using is made-up, and you can't get in trouble for impersonating someone who doesn't actually exist."

I often wondered if a business like mine would have worked in, say, Wheeling, West Virginia. Wouldn't more suspicious people in Wheeling hang up on me or call 911? I suppose I'll never know. But in a tough place like New York, where people are always looking for a leg up, you could quickly win a client's admiration if they thought you had a clever idea, no matter how legal that idea might be.

I would often try to visualize what the picture of my "office" looked like in the caller's mind. Did they envision secretaries and carpeting and white enamel desks? Was there someone making coffee or gossiping around a water cooler? One of the keys to my success would be to establish credibility with my clients, enough that they'd consent to giving me their credit card number over the phone to buy their ticket. If I could give the impression of being in a busy office, my task would be far more easily accomplished.

"Could you hold a moment?" I'd ask, for no good reason.

There's nothing like making somebody hold, to give the impression of being busy; though, in my case, there was always an obligatory bit of holding I had to impose on my clients each day, when I went to the bathroom, because the flushing sound in the tiny apartment was deafening and, consequently, bad for business. Not having any employees, I had to answer every call myself, even if I was indisposed when the phone rang. Putting the person on hold until I wasn't indisposed served the dual purpose of building their confidence and relieving my bladder.

"How do I know you'll give me the money for the boarding

pass?" they'd ask.

"You don't. Except that I'm telling you I will, you already know my phone number, and I'm not about to sacrifice my whole business for your fifty bucks. Besides, even if I did rip you off, you'd still only be paying the lowest available fare for your ticket."

It was a winning argument. Sometimes callers would say they wanted to think about it, but they'd inevitably call me back the same day, often within the next five minutes, which led me to believe that, rather than thinking about it, they wanted to seize the initiative in the matter, lest I think that I'd told them something they didn't already know. It's like that in New York.

In order to accumulate the mileage in a useful way, I opened a series of imaginary frequent flier accounts with each airline. Each ticket I bought and resold through my mother's agency had to have either Mr. or Ms. on it, per airline regulations, which I got around by putting all my accounts in non-gender specific names. Chris Lawson, Dana McIntyre, Shelly Richards. Anybody, male or female, could be any one of these people, and, indeed, many were—so many, in fact, that sometimes the airlines denied me credit for certain flights because Chris Lawson had flown from Los Angeles to Newark, New York to Miami, and Atlanta to Dallas, all at the same time. Not having a staff in my office, I lacked the manpower to double-check that no one's flight paths and times were impossibly crossing. Whenever I'd get turned down, I'd just play dumb, as in brain-damaged dumb. They would call Ms. Lawson (a.k.a. me) and ask how this was possible and I would say, in the most Chris-Lawson-as-innocent-and-brain-damaged-female voice I could muster: "Maybe the computer glitched."

Or I'd say: "I'd just like to get credit for the Los Angeles to Newark flight (the longest of the three) I took."

Occasionally I'd use a gruff male voice and dare them to challenge me on it. What could they say? You don't sound like a woman?

"Of course I don't, I'm not even an actual human being."

While I accumulated all these miles through my *Village Voice* ads, I was simultaneously hawking half-price first-class fares to Europe in *The Wall Street Journal*. Since a passport was required for international travel, those tickets had to be issued in the name of the real person traveling. Luckily, the airlines allowed you to transfer your awards to a "relative." Thus, if you wanted to buy one of these tickets from me, you were no longer just a client. You became my cousin. I had more cousins than the Sultan of Brunei. In the end, for my investment of about $500 (ten roundtrip tickets coast-to-coast at $50 each) I'd have enough miles to get a first-class award I could sell for $3000. And a new relative to boot.

Things got dodgy at times. Once, a frantic phone call came from one of my clients at the airport. He was supposed to fly to Los Angeles, but he'd run into a problem.

"They took my ticket!"

"Who took your ticket?"

"The guy at check-in. He asked me for ID, and when I said I didn't have any, he wrote 'Must Show ID' across my ticket!"

"So he gave you your ticket back."

"Yes. But he wrote 'must show ID' on it."

This was a real dilemma. No one had ever asked for ID before. I told my client to call me back in five minutes, then picked up the phone and called the one criminal mastermind I knew well.

"Mom? I have a client at the airport who got asked for ID. The ticket agent wrote, 'must show ID' on his ticket."

"What color ink did he write in?" she asked, without a moment's hesitation.

"I don't know, Mom. Blue, I guess."

"Tell him to get a blue pen and cross it out. Then have him check in again with the same ticket at the curbside check-in."

"You're kidding me."

"Don't worry, Michael. It'll work."

"Are you crazy? What if it doesn't work?" my terrified client asked, five minutes later.

"Trust me, it'll work," I said. *Because my mommy said it would*, I thought, but chose not to say.

That was the last I heard of the guy until he got back from his trip. He actually wound up recommending me to a whole host of his friends.

Christmas was a special time of year for exploiters of loopholes in the airline system like me. Flights were packed, and I'd always have trouble finding seats for my passengers seeking to fly home for the holidays. But it was this overcrowded scenario that soon gave birth to a new idea—a kind of travel jujitsu in which I'd try to get paid *not* to fly.

Airlines lose money when they have empty seats on their planes. So, in order to mitigate those losses and to capitalize on the fickleness of travelers, they routinely overbook their flights. They know some people will inevitably cancel, others will change their itineraries, and others will oversleep and miss their flights. They never truly know how many passengers they have for each flight until everyone has checked in. If they are still overbooked when the flight is close to boarding, they make an announcement such as this:

"We are offering a coupon good for $200 in air travel, as well as a guaranteed seat on our next flight out, to anyone who will voluntarily give up their seat."

Usually, cash-strapped students, hardcore bargain hunters, and people in no particular hurry offer to put their names on the volunteer list. When the final seat count is determined, some or all of the volunteers are given coupons and put on the next flight, while everyone else leaves on the current outgoing flight as planned. If not enough volunteers materialize, the offer is raised, sometimes as high as $1000, until a sufficient number of seats open up. Given that kind of payoff, some people consider themselves lucky to be bumped.

But there's an old saying that luck comes to those who best prepare for it. I decided to prepare myself for this particular brand of serendipity by buying tickets on all the flights I expected to be overbooked around Christmas. Tickets back then were refundable if you changed your mind and decided not to fly. The difference in my case was that I, and a few enterprising friends who also bought tickets with me, had already made up our minds. We went to Kennedy Airport the day before Christmas, and the day before that, too, with our tickets in hand. We then waited for the overbooking announcements to begin, in the hopes of volunteering our pre-reserved seats on the flight. But like any scam, this one too had its own special nuances. If you agreed to be a volunteer for $200, you lost the chance to be a volunteer at $400 or higher if the bid went up. At the same time, if too many volunteers signed up before you, you risked being left out altogether. Thus, we all pretended to loiter close to the service desk at the gate, so as to be within hearing range of the flight agents as they monitored the number volunteers signing up and spaces available.

The times when it worked, we humbly accepted our coupons and nodded gratefully as the agents reserved our seats on the ensuing flights, which we would not be taking either. We were too busy trying to volunteer ourselves off other overbooked flights elsewhere in the terminal.

Yet, despite the Christmas rush, overbooking sometimes worked out in the airline's favor even then. Enough seats would be available for everyone who had come for the flight, which presented us with the delicate task of having to instantly invent an excuse for not wanting to take the flight, so we could refund our tickets. Back then, there were no cell phones, so we couldn't just pretend to receive an urgent phone call about a sudden family emergency. Thus, we resorted to shaking our heads slowly, as though channeling unseen imprecations, and saying things like, "You know, I suddenly have a really bad feeling about this flight. May I please refund my ticket?"

"Yeah, me too."

"Me, too."

None of us were superstitious, of course. We knew that air travel was far safer than traveling by car, but I never felt like I was truly acting because I'd become so used to never being the person whose name was on my plane ticket. Thus, it never felt like I was actually the person who was claiming to be afraid to fly. My doppelganger was. *I would be happy to fly*, I would think to myself. *It is Chris Lawson who doesn't want to go.*

Before long, I began to face competition in the mileage accumulation business, from companies whose expensive advertisements I'd see in *The New York Times*. I'd call them to see what they were offering, and usually it was the same deal as mine, only they had *real* offices, with hired personnel and water coolers. They also had a quality that I have sorely lacked in my life: a voracious appetite for profit. There were times that I'd think: *why don't I do like them, and hire some people, advertise more, and try to create a business in which I'll make a lot of money without really having to work much?* In retrospect, I think I had a post-liberal-arts hangover from college. I still considered myself a communist. I was more likely to begin a campaign to nationalize the airlines before I'd go headlong into business as a capitalist. And, before I knew it, circumstances beyond my control made the decision for me.

The airlines started cracking down on mileage accumulation businesses, which were now referring to themselves as "mileage brokers." A few carriers took some of my competitors to court. While the airlines were never able to win any sort of prosecutions, since nothing anyone had done was technically illegal, they began carefully scrutinizing flight patterns and regularly denying mileage credit to the "we-went-to-three-places-at-the-same-time" crowd, like my imaginary relatives and me. In short order, I sold off my remaining first-class tickets and called it a career. The following day, my phone rang one last time.

"Hello, Michael?"

"Yes."

"This is Tom Jason from the California Student Loan Commission."

I still owed several thousand dollars on loans I'd taken as a college student, and I'd managed for several years—until that very moment actually—to avoid paying them back. My inner-commie-pinko felt that education should be free, and not paying back my loans had been my feeble attempt to render it so. But the jig was now up.

Jason found me by calling my mother in California and pretending to be an old college friend who'd lost touch with me and wanted to reconnect. The great criminal mastermind fell for his ruse and gave him my number in New York.

"Tell me who to make the check out to," I said. "I've finally got the money."

# FRENCH LESSON

**Jackie Strawbridge**

"Non. Imagine you
Are chewing chocolate."
She dropped her tongue
And chin, clapped
Her chalked hands and
Pointed to her mouth.
"Aah," she oozed. Paused
And then repeated, "aah,"
Then "ooh, ee," letting
The thick vowels drip.
Swinging her jaw
Like a sedated horse
Trying to graze. "Essayez!"

"S'il vous plait, madame,
Je cherche le canal."
She blinked, puffed out
Her cheeks. "Comment?"
I sighed and tried again,
Still spitting impossible
Syllables like unpopped
Corn kernels. "Le canal?"
"Il est où?" I swung
Out my arms, rowing
An invisible boat,
To convey water.
"Oh!" She clapped.
"Vous voulez dire
"Canal," vowels

Gurgling from her nose.
She raised her palms
And together we sang,
"Canal, canal." She nodded
Down a dim-lit road
And I approached it.

# MY OWN SPECIAL CAVIAR

**Yvonne Pesquera**

It was week two of our backpacking trip through Russia and I had not checked off "eat caviar" on my list of things to do. I panicked. Ed and I were set to depart Russia that evening, by overnight train to Finland.

With an additional four more weeks to go on our backpacking itinerary, Ed and I were straining under the weight of spending all of our time together in what is just a modestly comfortable country.

But today was a good day. We selected a small, dusty railway town on the outskirts of St. Petersburg as our point of departure from Russia. The town square had a museum and an onion-domed church—and was small enough so we could walk off from one another's sight without worrying about the other.

I poked my head in to a café that didn't look too touristy or too clean. I struggled with the Cyrillic letters on the menu, but finally made out what looked like "caviar."

At the time of our visit, the exchange rate was a highly favorable one dollar to 33 rubles. When I saw that the caviar cost was 99 rubles, I was overjoyed to do the conversion and realize that pure Russian caviar would only cost me three bucks. With a Francophile history that runs very deep, Russians prefer French as the tourist language. So, in my best French, I pointed to the caviar listing and simply told him I wanted it in French. "Je voudrais, s'il vous plaît."

The waiter reviewed my matted hair, that hadn't seen conditioner in weeks; and then he let his eyes drift down my rumpled, borscht-stained travel shorts and hideous, yet reliable, Teva sandals.

I pulled out a crisp 100 ruble note and placed it on the table before he could utter, "Nyet." He grunted, lit a cigarette, and disappeared behind the kitchen curtain.

Looking out the café window, I opened my *Lonely Planet* to

read about the 18th century church that Ed was heading toward, across the pigeon-filled square, and wondered if my food would come out fast enough for me to join him. But before I made it past the introductory paragraph, Ed came hustling in to the café, with his backpack slowing his motion like a parasail.

Breathlessly, he said, "The church guardian will unlock the gates for us."

"So?" I asked. The guardians were always keeping the doors locked so that visitors would pay them a ruble to get in.

Actually, we were lucky if it would just cost us a ruble. If we were unlucky, the keyholder would ask for a personal possession. It'd been over a decade since the USSR dissolved into the Russian Federation, but, still, *Amerika*—spelled with a k—was the Promised Land. And any of our belongings—no matter how trivial: my comb, Ed's floss—were highly prized.

"But this church has a saint in it," he explained.

I threw my arms up in the air because now his excited state made sense.

*

The Russians are particularly fond of displaying their dead people. In the Kremlin's Red Square, I gamely stood in the presence of the very dead and highly embalmed Vladimir Lenin. I forgave the country for this morbid exhibit because I thought it was Russia's version of "Disneyland" for the tourists.

But in nearly every church I've visited since, there were "relics"— meaning the fingers, ears, and toes—of revered saints proudly on display. And the better churches had their actual dead saints lying encased in plastic (but not in a special airlock Plexiglas like Lenin) and without the expensive post-mortem treatment to prevent decay (like Lenin); which was a great source of consternation for me because some of these saints' bodies were 100 years old and their toes curled backward and their fingers gnarled forward, usually blackened and broken off at the first joint, and their faces were not peaceful at all in encountering Jesus—not because Heaven isn't great, but because the people of the great Federation of Russia won't let their dead rest in peace.

Before I could utter a protest, which was actually a wish not to see another dead person before we crossed the border in just two hours, Ed cried, "What the hell did you order?"

With my back to the waiter, he was the first to see my lunch coming out of the kitchen. It was not the tight, black Petrossian caviar I had spooned onto toast points at cocktail parties in New York. Nor was it the bright red roe that peppered my sashimi in Tokyo's sushi bars.

No, this was a seething mound of coral-pink fish eggs, piled high in a goop that was meant to be a sauce, and, to my horror, it seemed that the eggs were still moving. Nothing in this country was properly dead.

I shocked the waiter by preventing him from placing the dish in front of me. I gestured toward the back kitchen and rudely shouted in French for him to go, "Allez, allez!" because there was no other polite French phrase I could quickly muster.

The church guardian rapped on the café window. Even though his bony wrist was bare, he pointed to an imaginary watch, gestured toward the train station, and then swept his arms toward the church the like the late P.T. Barnum.

Ed said, "We have to go. This is our last chance."

If only my café meal had been a halfway decent crepe or a bowl of porridge, I could have easily deflected the visit and made a defensible case for my nourishment. But knowing that that freak show of a horror plate was still moving behind the curtain, I threw down an extra ruble and bolted for the door.

But the waiter commanded me to stop and handed me the caviar in a take-out container with a clear plastic see-through lid. There are no street trashcans throughout Russia. And there is also no anonymity. So, between the town square and the train depot, I'd have no chance of ditching this plate of live fish eggs without being seen and having it reported back to the waiter. The last thing you want to do in a small town anywhere, but particularly in Russia, is offend anyone. And I was already borderline on that.

In a stroke of genius, I offered the plate of fish eggs to the church guardian who recoiled at the sight with head-shaking and several "Nyets." Ed had to offer the guy a pen we had picked up from an Amex currency exchange office, and we were whisked inside. Within moments, we were standing in front of a plastic case with two women saints whose arms were supposed to be placidly crossed on their chests, but because of the brittle state of the corpses, had broken and now stood out at angles that resembled a stack of fire kindling.

At this point, I just wanted to crawl into the plastic box next to them.

We heard the train whistle blow and gathered our packs, took two last photos of a Virgin Mary icon, and tried, once again, to offer my plate to the church guardian. But he declined and said in perfect English to me, "Amerika good!"

On the train that evening to Helsinki, as soon as the locomotion really got under way and we were in the hinterlands of countryside between borders, we opened the train car window and sailed the plate of fish eggs into the high grasses.

The Russian Border Patrol banged on our car door, for their usual inspection of passports, and I was laughing so hard from throwing the fish eggs back into Russia that I shouted to the guards, "One second; I'm burying your dead!" and the guard shouted back through the closed doors: "Please speak in French, Madam!"

# A CONVERSATION WITH MICHAEL C. KEITH

***Lowestoft Chronicle*, January 2013**

Michael C. Keith (photography: Lee Nadel)

His memoir, *The Next Better Place*, described by *Publishers Weekly* as "a hitchhiker travelogue that reads like Little League Kerouac," has been likened to *Angela's Ashes* and praised by the likes of Larry King and Augusten Burroughs. His short stories have received praise from iconic science fiction writer Ray Bradbury and *The Huffington Post*. Surprisingly, Michael C. Keith is actually better known for his scholarly books on broadcast media, radio in particular. He has authored some two dozen books on electronic media, one of which, *The Radio Station*, is the most widely adopted textbook on radio in America, and *Waves of Rancor: Tuning in the Radical Right*, which he coauthored with Robert L. Hilliard, was on President Clinton's summer reading list.

Recently, *Lowestoft Chronicle* caught up with Michael C. Keith to discuss his poignant and comic memoir, his fiction and academic works, and his literary tastes and influences.

**Lowestoft Chronicle (LC):** *The Next Better Place* is a brazen account of your travels across America with your father, Curt, in 1959 (from Pittsburgh to Indianapolis, Denver to Los Angeles, Las Vegas to Fort Worth, and back to Albany). How would you describe the process of writing the book, and what made you decide to tell the story from the perspective of an eleven-year-old?

The Next Better Place | Algonquin | 2003

**Michael C. Keith (MCK):** The process was an ongoing and lengthy one. I had it in mind to write about my unique childhood from the time I became an adult, but it took decades before it was ripe for the telling and then only after outline after outline. The writing went through several stages. The memoir first manifested in the form of an ill-conceived screenplay (one is currently being written by a professional screenwriter), then it became a full-length manuscript with prologue and epilogue, and finally it morphed into a penultimate version, sans prologue and epilogue. I had sent it out to tons of publishers and agents, and you know how that story goes. Finally, I sent it to the agent of a friend, and they liked it. After a dozen rejections, it was picked up by Algonquin Books. That was an exciting day, to say the least. You really get to the point that you think it will never be sold. Having it contracted by a prestige house like Algonquin was the frosting on the cake, and my editor there turned out to be fantastic. She really related to the story because she had a young son. So once it found a home, things went very smoothly. Searching for and finding that home was almost a greater challenge than writing the book.

Actually, the writing went well once I recognized what needed to be done to the manuscript to make it salable. I had this overwrought vision about telling the story of my entire life by employing a lengthy (windy) prologue and epilogue. That was a mistake. The core of the manuscript was *the* book. The prologue and epilogue just got in the way of the essential story. It took quite a while for me to realize that. I well remember the day I realized what had to be done. It was an epiphany of sorts. I was walking across the Boston College campus on my way to teach, and it suddenly occurred to me that I had to dump the front and back matter in the manuscript. At that same moment, the title came to me, too—*The Dream of Motion*. I loved that title, but my editor thought it sounded like the title of a book about running. She suggested a phrase from the book—*The Next Better Place*—and it became the title. I still prefer *The Dream of Motion*, but I suspect I made a wise concession.

As far as deciding from what perspective to tell the story, that was a non-issue. From the start, I knew it should be told by my eleven-year-old self. It seemed recounting the experience from a child's point of view would allow me to get the most out of the narrative. The child is just old enough to see the world as both a scary and wondrous place. That combination gives you a lot to work with. Initially, I feared it would be very difficult to capture the mindset of an eleven-year-old, but it turned out to be a very natural and easy writing experience. Maybe having a stunted maturity helps—I jest (hopefully).

**LC:** When not on a Greyhound bus, daily life revolves around flophouses and homeless missions, beleaguered by perverts and lowlifes, or getting into trouble (at one point, you're charged as an accomplice to an armed robbery). Considering the hardships you faced on your travels—the constant hunger, your routine disappointment in your father, your grim surroundings, and the cast of sleazy characters you meet—did you find it difficult to write about your experiences in *The Next Better Place*?

**MCK:** Not as you might think. Having lived with the experience for so long, I gained some distance and was able to view it with a certain objectivity. It all seemed like a quirky road movie to me as I got older. Fortunately, my father was a pretty benign guy, who, in his strange way, tried to look after me. Despite some gloomy periods involving his drinking and my hunger, it seemed like a high adventure to me. I had the kind of freedom few kids have, and that appealed to me. No school, no bedtimes, no baths more than compensated for the rough spots. Many times during the writing process, I laughed out loud recalling the ridiculousness of some of our situations. Maybe humor is a good way to cope with the bizarre. The reaction of readers is interesting. Generally speaking, women seem to view my situation as a kid with sadness and sympathy, while men often see it as plain funny and strange. It was certainly all of those things and a good deal more.

LC: In terms of closure, the book ends with the reader speculating about many things—did you continue on to Florida with Curt, or did the journey end in Albany? After your return home, what became of Curt, and how would you describe your relationship with him? What impact did these travels have on the rest of your life?

MCK: Actually, the paperback version, that published a year after the hardcover, has an outcomes chapter. We did head out to Florida, and for the next several years, continued our gypsy-style life. I broke away at seventeen when I convinced my father to sign me in to the army. Best thing I ever did. Helped me put things in perspective and gave me a better understanding of what my life with my father had been about. He continued to drink, but no matter how old I was, he always remained close by. There was a definite attachment, if not dependency, on me. I often bailed him out of tight situations caused by his alcoholism. On the brighter side, he often helped babysit my daughter, who developed a close relationship with him. It was a sort of redemption for him, but I always felt a level of anger for his depriving me of a normal childhood. In the end, though, my uncommon childhood may have had a positive impact on me in the sense that it provided me with a great model of how not to conduct one's life.

LC: Why didn't you write a further memoir about your travel experiences, and is there any possibility that you will do in the future?

MCK: The idea of a sequel has been in the back of my mind since the publication of *The Next Better Place*. It is, at the moment, being adapted for the screen by an LA screenwriter with some credentials, but as I'm sure you realize, getting anything to screen is a real long shot. Unfortunately, the book only did modestly well in terms of sales (although it was a critical success), so Algonquin is not keen on a sequel. They have encouraged me to write a novel, and that I may do some day.

LC: I'm surprised to hear you say *The Next Better Place* wasn't a commercial success, considering the extensive media exposure it got and the fact there's also an audio version available.

MCK: As fate would have it, the book was released the first day of the so-called *"Shock and Awe."* Turns out the start of the Iraqi War impacted book sales and kept people too preoccupied to buy books for a while. At least that's the prevailing wisdom. The book made enough to pay back my advance, so I suspect around five thousand copies were sold. Not sure about that figure, but it seems to calculate. It was a disappointment, because we all thought it would do better. Apparently, it did well enough for Algonquin to publish it in paperback, and now it's in ebook format (Kindle and Nook), so it lives on. And there is the possibility of a film version someday.

LC: There's a moment in the book when you're listening to a radio show (Don McNeill's *Breakfast Club*) in a boardinghouse, and you say to one of the boarders, "I'm going to be on the radio someday, too." Surprisingly, this is one of the few references to radio in the entire book. Did radio play a significant role in your childhood? What made you want to be a radio broadcaster, and how did you get involved in that field?

MCK: Radio was ubiquitous in the 1950s, so even in the flophouses, there often was an old radio to listen to. It became one of my primary forms of entertainment and distraction. It also served as a companion when my father wasn't around. I would often fantasize being on the radio, so I guess it was no surprise that I would consider a career behind the microphone. As soon as I was discharged from the service, I went to radio school. After getting my certificate, I got a job at a small New Hampshire station as an announcer and, from there, worked my way into larger markets. I spent a dozen years in the medium in various jobs: production director, newsman, account executive. Eventually, I longed for something different and went to college on the G.I. Bill. Many years later, I became a college professor and am now nearing retirement after thirty-five years in the classroom teaching communication studies. During that satisfying period, I wrote several books on electronic media, mainly centered on the cultural aspects of radio.

**LC:** *Voices in the Purple Haze: Underground Radio and the Sixties*, is an interesting account of the rise and fall of commercial underground radio, which rejected established structures of Top 40 radio. Evolving around 1966, it peaked between 1967 and 1969, before fading in 1971. Studio memorandums, station mandates, and sample playlists aside, your book is largely comprised of interviews with 32 prominent figures of freeform radio in the U.S. What made you decide to write about this very brief counterculture movement? How challenging was the process of rounding up so many of these radio personalities and getting them to share with you their opinions? And were there any radio practitioners (Tom Gamache, Bob Fass, Larry Yurdin, Buck Matthews, and Bob McClay, for example) that you wish you could have interviewed, but didn't get the chance?

**MCK:** I'm a youth of the 60s and a radio scholar, and so the role of the medium during that period fascinated me. I also knew that the story would be much better told by the people who lived it. As an old radio guy, I had a number of contacts, which led to other contacts, etc. Soon I had a marvelous bunch of underground radio pioneers to draw from. Of course, there's always someone you miss, but I'm quite satisfied that the people I got very comprehensively represented this unusual and unique form of radio. Of all the monographs I did in the area of radio studies, this is one of my favorites. The frosting on the cake was that the book was very well-received by the underground radio community.

**LC:** *The Radio Station* is your most successful book and considered a seminal book on radio broadcasting? Can you explain why the book has proved to be so popular?

**MCK:** Up until the time *The Radio Station* was published in 1986, radio books were fairly bland and, often, somewhat dated in their focus. That is to say, they were short on visuals and out of touch with the realities of the contemporary radio marketplace. I conceived a text that would show as well as tell and tell from the perspective of industry people. It was a formula that worked, and *The Radio Station* became the most widely used text on its subject in the country. It's also used throughout the world, and because of that, I've been invited to lecture in Russia, Indonesia, Spain, etc. Now it's about to morph into *Keith's Radio Station*, co-authored by two excellent media academics. I reached a point after producing eight editions of the text that I no longer cared to continue, but the publisher did. So now I have my name in the title, and that is very gratifying.

**LC:** Having published three short story collections recently, have you moved away from academic writing to focus on fiction, or do you have another nonfiction book in the pipeline?

**MCK:** Actually, *four* story collections. My newest, *Sad Boy*, was just published by Big Table Publishing, an excellent small press. I tired of writing academic books (thirty-two volumes in all) so sought refuge in fiction about six years ago, starting with a young adult novel, *Life is Falling Sideways*. After it, I became involved in short story writing and found I had somewhat of a facility for it. Now, here I sit with 130 stories published (with several writing award nominations) and contemplating what's next. I'm sure more short stories are in my future, but longer form fiction is likely up the road, too. That said, part of me thinks: *keep writing short stories and maybe someday you'll get really good at it*. That's a worthy objective, but I get itchy to try other things.

**LC:** I've heard you say in an interview that TV shows like *The Outer Limits*, *The Twilight Zone*, and *Science Fiction Theatre* influenced you growing up. Were there any particular writers, books, or magazines that shaped your writing?

**MCK:** B horror and sci-fi movies were also an influence. Among authors most intriguing me at a young age, I'd say Ray Bradbury, Kurt Vonnegut, Isaac Asimov, and Stephen King (later on) had some influence on me. However, again in the interest of full disclosure, I must admit that I was never a big reader of speculative fiction or short stories. I liked novels featuring contemporary humor, irony, and angst. Always loved Philip Roth and John Irving, to name only a couple. Back in the day—when I had flowers in my hair—I was a fan of Richard Brautigan. The literary genre I like best is biography (mostly about authors), even ahead of fiction.

**LC:** I hear the dark novella you're working on is an extended version of the short story "The Waiting Bell" (published in *Sleet Magazine*). Is this correct? What made you want to develop this story and why a novella?

**MCK:** You are quite correct—you have good spies. The story idea came to me when I read an article about the waiting houses in Germany during the 19th century plague. It struck me as a wonderful idea to spin into a Gothic horror story. That bodies were actually stored in warehouses until it was determined beyond a doubt that they were dead absolutely intrigued me. Stories that come about through casual encounters are a real gift from the writing gods. I've had many such encounters and consider myself lucky for it. "The Waiting Bell" turned out to be one of my stronger stories. People really had an emotional reaction to it. Rereading it recently, the idea for a full-length treatment came to me. Much is already outlined, so I'll see if it really does lend itself to the novella format. I hope it does.

**LC:** How would you describe your latest book, *Sad Boy*? How does this book differ from your last three short story collections?

**MCK:** I think *Sad Boy* is a bit mellower and somewhat less speculative than my previous collections in that the stories take place more in the so-called realm of reality. Of course, some are way beyond the boundaries of reality, but many deal with males facing challenging *real*-life situations and issues. That said, *Sad Boy* is filled with some pretty twisty/twisted tales. I can't help that because I have a pretty twisty/twisted creative imagination. Besides, who wants to write about real life? Much of it is too mundane for my pen. As a sad (old) boy myself, I'm drawn to write about those dark corners.

**LC:** What inspired "Gertrude's Grave," your latest short story for *Lowestoft Chronicle*? How did this macabre tale come about?

**MCK:** I've been doing a lot of reading about the Lost Generation lately, so Gertrude Stein was on my mind. I decided to look up where she was buried and discovered it was in Paris. After that, one thought led to another. That's kind of how most of my stories manifest. Something triggers my curiosity and the race is on. I guess that's true of many writers. Thank God for Google. Given the weirdness of many of my tales, I think of the Internet search engine as the "Wizard of Odd." It's a great and powerful resource.

# GERTRUDE'S GRAVE

**Michael C. Keith**

> Gertrude has said things tonight it will take her 10 years to understand. — Alice B. Toklas

A passage from Ernest Hemingway's memoir, *A Moveable Feast*, never left Otto Niemeyer's thoughts: "If you are lucky enough to have lived in Paris as a young man, then wherever you go for the rest of your life, it stays with you, for Paris is a moveable feast." He had never been to Paris, but he had always hoped to go. His salary as a geography teacher at Jarvis Wile School in Summit, Missouri, had never provided him with the funds necessary to make the trip. Private schools in his part of the world were notoriously cheap to their faculty. It was only after putting aside money from a part-time job at an auto parts store, following his retirement, that he was finally able to realize his long delayed dream.

Otto planned to visit the haunts of the book's iconic expats. He would patronize the cafes of Montparnasse, where Hemingway, Fitzgerald, Joyce, and other legendary figures spent long evenings of drinking and jousting with each other. He'd retrace their paths across the City of Lights, and he'd visit the graves of Gertrude Stein and Alice B. Toklas in the Père Lachaise Cemetery. Of all the characters in Hemingway's reminiscences, Stein and Toklas held a special fascination for him. It was their devotion to one another that most caught his fancy. That the two women had found each other, in a world hostile to unconventional couplings, had given him hope. Although he was straight, their relationship served as a beacon in the lonely sea of his existence. A lifelong bachelor, Otto had spent his entire adulthood without a significant other.

While he was not a big fan of Stein's prose style—*What the hell did* "There ain't no answer. There ain't gonna be any answer. There never has been an answer. That's the answer," or "There is no there there" *mean?* He did enjoy her apparent playfulness with words, but was nonplussed by their ambiguity or, perhaps, it was his lack of comprehending their intended meaning. Still, he admired her deeply and truly looked forward to paying homage to her and the woman who had been her closest consort. The idea that he would be in such close proximity to their remains thrilled him and gave him a sense that he might somehow become a part of their fabled oeuvre.

While his knowledge of the French language was modest, he felt confident it would not pose a problem and, despite his arthritic knees, they were still capable of withstanding hearty walks. It was in this heightened frame of mind that Otto boarded a plane to New York that would connect with a flight to France. He could not have been happier, and he uncharacteristically engaged with as many fellow travelers as he could to share his joy. It was one of the brightest times in his life—a life that had been awash in monotones of grey. Even his childhood, with older parents, had been a lackluster and unmemorable affair. Like Otto, his mother and father had also taught at Jarvis Wile School their entire careers, and like him, they, too, had been forced to stay close to home because of a lack of resources to do otherwise.

*

The day after arriving in Paris, Otto took a cab to the Père Lachaise Cemetery. He had first planned to visit the Eiffel Tower and the Louvre, but his powerful urge to visit the resting place of his literary heroines prompted him to revise his plan. After being deposited at the tree-enshrouded entrance of the graveyard, Otto began to stroll down the main path. He was surprised to see how crammed the gravestones were to one another. He had never seen such a crowded burial ground and was glad he had purchased a map of the site in advance of his visit. It would have been impossible to achieve his purpose otherwise, he concluded. The map included information about the graveyard that amazed Otto. More than 70,000 resided in this city of the dead spread over more than one hundred acres. The 5,000 trees lining the gravel lanes delighted him, and the shadows they cast were stenciled to the ground by a vibrant June sun. The effect was captivating and almost otherworldly to Otto, and he could not conceive of a lovelier place to spend the hereafter.

*I'm coming, dear Gertrude*, he thought excitedly, as he checked the directory on the back of the map labeled "Noted Occupants." He quickly ran his finger down the long alphabetized column. *There she is.* He could hardly contain his excitement when he came to her name. I'm coming, *Le Stein*, said Otto, using the sobriquet given to her by her celebrated coterie. When he reached the grande dame's grave, he was surprised and somewhat disappointed by how unadorned it appeared set next to a small, yellow storage building. *Oh, même moderne, you deserve better*, he mumbled to himself, as he knelt close to her headstone. "How you must long for your beloved *Rue de Fleurus*," he whispered sympathetically.

As Otto backed away from the decrepit monument, he was certain he heard a female voice intone, "A grave is grave unless it is not grave." *Yes*, he thought, *yes, of course, dear Gertrude. How could one be grave among friends and lovers? Now, those words I understand. Merci, Le Stein.*

Referring to the plot directory again to find the Toklas site, he suddenly became aware that they were just two of a myriad of renowned fellow tenants. He had been so focused on locating Stein that he had failed to see who else was interred in the sacred ground around her. His eyes widened in amazement as they ran down the list: Apollinaire, Balzac, Bernhardt, Bizet, Calas, Chopin, Debussy, Delacroix, Ernst, Pisarro, Seurat . . . Otto was overcome with the realization that he stood among the remains of some of the world's most renowned cultural figures. He immediately became obsessed with the idea of becoming an occupant of the hallowed necropolis upon his passing. *It would be so wonderful to spend eternity with such extraordinary people. I must . . . I must.*

*

Over the next several days, Otto paid his respects to many of the other famous occupants of Père Lachaise. He had also contacted its office to inquire about the possibility of being buried there. The cost of purchasing a plot was formidable, however, and was laden with conditions. An individual had to die in Paris in order to be eligible and sign a renewable lease of 10, 30, or 50 years—the longer the lease, the more expensive. Since plots were limited, if a lease expired, the remains would be removed and relocated. A body could be cremated and placed in the cemetery's columbarium for less expense, but that did not appeal to Otto. His deepest wish was to share the cemetery's soil with its deceased luminaries. He believed that to rest among them would add meaning and weight to his otherwise jejune existence.

Otto figured that in order to purchase the plot, he would have to do something drastic to raise the money, and he knew what that meant. He would have to sell his mother's engagement ring, which he had inherited long ago. The formidable diamond had been handed down through generations of Niemeyers and was worth a considerable sum. While it disturbed him to depart with it, he justified doing so since there had never been anyone to give it to. He had not married and the prospects of getting engaged at his age were less than remote.

He put a down payment on the plot with a credit card, agreeing to pay the balance within thirty days, and returned to the States feeling positively exuberant. While Otto had little to look forward to in what remained of his daily life, he now believed that, in death, he would achieve fulfillment. Spending eternity with the great and glorious was far better than living in his mundane world.

*

Otto located a buyer for his mother's ring, and to his satisfaction, the sum it brought was in excess of the money he needed to pay off his gravesite. He put the balance in the bank in anticipation of an eventual return trip to Paris when he felt his demise was nearing. Fearing that he might suffer a fatal accident before his time came, he substantially decreased his already nominal presence in the outside world by remaining in his small house as much as possible.

Thus, the years passed slowly and without notable incident until he suffered a minor heart attack. That prompted him to execute his long-planned end-of-days strategy.

"You need a repair of your left ventricle. It's a delicate operation, but you should come out of it okay, Mr. Niemeyer," said a coronary specialist at Summit Hospital, where he had been taken.

Upon hearing the doctor's words, the seventy-six year old patient decided to sell off everything he owned and cash in his retirement investments for his return to Paris. Immediately, after his release from the hospital, Otto set about to clear the path back to the Père Lachaise Cemetery for his rendezvous with Stein and her distinguished neighbors.

*Je reviendrai bientot, Le Stein*, thought Otto, and *soon* it was. Within two months, Otto had rented a small room near the cemetery in the 20th Arrondissement. While it cost considerably more than his previous dwelling in the poorer 19th Arrondissement, Otto felt that, since his days were numbered, his finances would more than suffice for the time that remained. He was surprised and a bit chagrined when months passed and his health did not deteriorate as he expected it would.

*

Indeed, the better part of a year passed while Otto impatiently waited for his end to come. During that time, he had visited Père Lachaise nearly every day and had long conversations with many of the cemetery's notables. Of course, among the most loquacious was Gertrude herself, who regaled him with countless anecdotes and tales of the Lost Generation. Otto could not wait to enter the afterlife with such intriguing and engaging friends. But his wait felt endless until the day before his birthday.

On his brief walk to the cemetery up a narrow street, Otto encountered two intimidating looking youths.

"You American, huh?"

Otto attempted to ignore them and continue on his way, but his path was blocked.

"Give us your things now! *Je te tuerai!*" threatened the smaller of the two.

When Otto hesitated, the second youth pulled out a knife.

"*Actuellement!*" he growled.

Otto handed over his wallet, watch, and signet ring, and

expected the youths to leave him alone.

"Your *jaquette*. What is there?"

"Nothing. Just some papers of no value," answered Otto, hoping they would not take the cemetery lease that he always carried with him in the event of the fatal heart attack he expected at any time.

"Give them to us!" demanded his assailants, rifling through his pockets and removing the papers.

"Please, they are worthless," pleaded Otto.

"*Non, un vieil homme!*" replied the teenager clutching the cemetery lease.

Both young men then turned and ran with Otto in slow pursuit.

"Keep everything, but give me back those papers!" shouted Otto in the direction of their vanishing figures.

As he lumbered across the street, he became dizzy and fell, striking his head against the curb with great force. And it was there that he died.

When the police examined his body, the only identification they found was an address on the elderly man's medical alert bracelet. After French officials contacted authorities in the States, Otto's remains were returned to Summit, Missouri. There he was buried with little fanfare in one of the town's two cemeteries. A modest headstone, engraved with just his first name, was placed next to Estelle and Harold Niemeyer's graves. Otto's parents had purchased the plot for their only child when he was born.

# THE VEGETABLE GODS

**George Moore**

In my garden, there are lambs
and griffins, the guardians of light
from older religions, and plaques

with bareheaded men, with women
turning away, the animals on four legs
condemned by scripture.

They prowling at night through
the carrots and peas, dancing on hind legs
whenever it rains.

In my garden, the water runs East to West,
without channel, culvert or ditch,
Jordan baptisms, a *Gathas* symbol of life

finds its way into the imprint
left by my foot.  The animals dive
and bring up mud to make a world.

In my garden, the vegetables bow
to an invisible *Priapos*, vegetal god laughing
at new-turned compost, applauded by goats and sheep.

Yet, in my garden, winter has stayed too long
for Proserpina's return, the days grow scaly
in geologic time, and I wait for the earth

to give up its fruits. The gods have never abandoned
their vines, but left furrows, traces as spring
dissolves with climate change,

a hot season rises up, a glimpse of hell,
and the animals wait for the gardener, a keeper of
the light, to carry them home to a new sun.

# RICE

**Ed Hamilton**

What I really wanted was a hamburger, but it seemed the only restaurant that was open on lower Haight Street was some trendy vegetarian joint. My girlfriend, Susan, liked to eat healthy, and she figured she could get a salad or something. It was early on a Sunday, before noon, and the place was pretty much deserted. As we took our seats in the booth, we noticed only one other couple sitting there amidst all the old dime store kitsch.

The waitress came out from behind the bar and gave us our menus. She was a twenty-something trendoid, probably just graduated from college, with a major in art or English, from the looks of her. She had her long hair dyed red with a white skunk stripe down the middle, and wore blue velvet bell-bottom hip huggers and an orange and blue belly shirt that looked like part of an old gas station uniform or something. She had the nose ring, the multiple earrings, and the navel ring. None too appetizing.

The girl had us pegged as tourists: "Where you folks from?" she asked.

"New York City," Susan told her.

"Ah, ha, ha!" the waitress laughed, and walked off.

"I don't think she believed us," Susan said.

"It's probably our southern accents," I suggested.

"And that blue jean jacket really makes you look like a hick."

"Thanks," I said.

As soon as the waitress went through the open door to the kitchen, she shrieked at the cook: "What are you doing?!"

Now I've worked in restaurants before, and the thing is, when you get back in the kitchen, you just assume that the customers can't hear you. And it's usually the case. Probably if there had been more people in the place, their noise would have drowned out the kitchen conversation.

"I'm just getting ready to boil up some rice," the cook said. We had seen him come out of the kitchen with a rack of glasses when we first walked in. He was a man of about thirty-five, with long brown hair. In his dirty jeans and t-shirt, he looked like a hippie.

"Do not throw that rice into that water," the waitress commanded. "Rice must be steamed."

"This is the way I always cook it."

"Then you have been doing it wrong. To properly cook rice, you must steam it."

"That's not going to work," the cook said.

"It most certainly will. The super-heated, pressurized steam moistens and tenderizes the rice," the waitress declared knowingly. "If you throw the rice down in the water, it will come out soggy and tough."

"Maybe there's just more than one way to do it," the cook tried to compromise. All those years without meat must have weakened his brain.

"Of course, there is more than one way. That much is obvious. However, my way is the right way."

"Well, I'm the cook."

"But I have an interest in this restaurant as well. I cannot very well serve my customers a substandard dish."

"All right," the cook said. "I've had enough of this. I'm not going to cook any rice at all. No rice today. People can just have potatoes or something else instead. Does that satisfy you?"

"Well, I suppose no rice is better than better than boiled rice," the waitress quipped snidely.

It was hard for me to believe that the cook had given in so easily. He should have screamed at her to get out of his kitchen, and threatened her with a skillet of hot grease. Most cooks I have known would not have hesitated for an instant before employing such means.

Now, the whole time this little melodrama had been going on in the kitchen, I had been looking at the menu, searching in vain for something halfway decent to order. And as I was doing so, I must have been making some pretty ugly faces, because Susan said, "Are you going to be able to find anything to eat here? If not, we may as well leave. The atmosphere doesn't seem that good anyway."

"Oh, no, no," I assured her. "Everything sounds great. It's just so hard to choose. And I really like this place. I want to stay."

Fresh off her triumph, the waitress bounced over to our table. "I've been to New York," she said. "I'm a playwright, you know."

So now she believed us. Or else she was just hedging her bets. Maybe she thought we might have been involved in the theater or something—and she didn't want to miss her big break.

"A theater there offered to produce my play," she continued, "but I told them I had too much going on here now."

"Good for you," I told her. "You should definitely stay here. This is a much more happening town."

It was time to order. For some reason, they didn't serve salads, at least not normal ones: all the dishes were vegetarian knockoffs of different kinds of southern food. So Susan ordered the Unchicken Cutlet (with mashed potatoes and cream gravy just the way your grandmother used to serve it).

"And you sir?" the waitress turned to me.

I couldn't help myself. There was nothing on the damn menu I wanted anyway. "Rice," I said.

"Excuse me?"

"I just want a big dish of rice. I'm on a special diet, and that's really all I like to eat." I knew she would go for the special diet line, since I figured plenty of lunatics and eccentrics probably came in there with all kinds of whacked-out requests.

The waitress tapped her pencil on her pad. "Well, it might take about twenty minutes. We haven't put the rice on yet."

"Oh, that's fine. I'll just smoke a cigarette or two in the meantime," I said. Even though it was sort of a health food place, they allowed smoking, I guess since cigarettes aren't made out of animals. They sold beer too. But not Budweiser. It's just not trendy enough. So I had a Heineken. Somebody really ought to figure out a way to make these products out of animals.

"I can't believe you did that," Susan whispered once the waitress got out of earshot.

"Hey, it's a vegetarian restaurant. They have to serve rice, so they might as well just work this problem out right here and now."

The waitress disappeared into the kitchen. "That man out there just ordered rice," she told the cook. "We need to get some going."

"I told you, no rice," the cook said.

"That's all he'll eat. Come on. I'll show you how to do it."

At this point I felt sure he would attack her with a cleaver like any normal, self-respecting cook. Instead, to my amazement, he still tried to reason with her.

"Listen, you don't know what you're talking about. I've been cooking rice since I was eight years old, since before you were born. I know how to do it. In the whole time I've been cooking here, no one's ever complained."

The waitress was unimpressed by the cook's credentials. "I learned how to cook rice from the Chinese," she proclaimed smugly. "They have been preparing rice for thousands of years."

"Fine!" the cook shouted. "You know so much, you do it yourself!"

The wisdom of the ancient Chinese had won out. Twenty minutes later, the waitress set the Unchicken Cutlet in front of Susan. Though I didn't tell Susan since I didn't want to ruin her meal, I knew beyond a shadow of a doubt that the cook had spat in grandmother's gravy. And then, a broad smile of satisfaction on her face, the waitress set my dish before me: a big, steaming plate of rice, garnished with some sort of leaves. Oh boy. Just what I wanted.

"Well, I hope you're pleased with yourself," Susan said once the waitress had gone. "You'd better eat every last bit of that, too."

Once again, I couldn't help myself. I signaled the waitress back over.

"Is there a problem, sir?"

"Yeah," I said. "I wanted this boiled."

# THE RISES AND FALLS OF SVETLANA HIPTOPSKI

**Kim Farleigh**

Svetlana Hiptopski was a successful model by the age of fifteen. The first time she wore sunglasses was in a Rome café; she was four years old; the glamour born from this fired such authentic affirmation through her that she knew, from then on, that being admired where the beautiful got observed and admired was her metier.

She adored chocolate-skinned Italians who swung deals on boats in Ibiza, Capri, and the Cayman Islands. A romance developed between her and the smouldering Italian fashion tycoon, Paulo Bombasini. Photographers snapped them in exotic locations. They could not have been happier.

"I travel light," Svetlana announced. "I take a credit card and buy what I need when I arrive."

Her delivery bills exceeded Somalia's GDP. She needed a lot. Crates rolled in from the Virgin Islands, Bali, Florida, Fiji, and Tahiti to her apartment beside the Eiffel Tower.

Federal Express's president said: "She travels light because planes can't fit her luggage."

"Buying when travelling," Svetlana said, "solves the problem of what to take."

Then disaster struck. Svetlana, after consuming Moet Chan don, slipped on Paulo's yacht's white-tiled bathroom floor, her head smacking gold faucets, in the Bay of Monte Carlo. The helicopter that whisked Svetlana and the fraught Paulo to a private clinic in Nice hadn't been flown in because of damage to Svetlana's impeccable appearance, but because of the now recondite expression that filled the basins of her opal eyes. She seemed oblivious; she didn't even recognise Paulo! The press were shocked: a woman was behaving as if the world's most eligible bachelor didn't even exist—a woman with a beguiling indifference toward Paulo Bombasini! The blow to Paulo's self-perception had the destructive force of a kilometer-wide tornado.

Clutching bedridden Svetlana's hand, Paulo quivered with agitation as he fought to induce a flicker of recognition from the now distant Svetlana, whose eyes converged at a point between Cuba and the Bahamas. Svetlana seemed to have lost all interest in buying clothes, shoes, and handbags: she hadn't mentioned shopping for five minutes!

Then Svetlana's lips twitched. Paulo thrust forward involuntarily. The tension would have made lesser men faint; but Paulo was made of cast iron—greased, of course, by ointments purchased on the Champs Élysées.

"I want to study the Roman Republic," Svetlana announced. "I want books about Julius Caesar."

Paulo rocked back aghast. He had been hoping for: "Oh, Paulo, I adore you," as if it had been him who had been suffering and who needed comforting.

The woman, whose normal reading material consisted of *Hello!* magazine and *Woman's Weekly*, was now intrigued by he whose crossing of the Rubicon transformed history.

"Really?" Paulo asked. "Darling, what is the problem?"

"I," she replied, esoterically, "suddenly feel...curious..."

"Curious?" Paulo replied.

"Yes," Svetlana said, observing that point between Cuba and the Bahamas. "It's amazing."

Paulo's conversation about Monaco's newest restaurants soon bored Svetlana, whose imagination had been awakened by a clash of champagne and gilded faucets. She told the hospital that she didn't want visitors as she devoured books on Roman history. The Eternal City now offered more than just shops and cafés.

Diamante Briatore, her agent, was so flabbergasted when Svetlana terminated her contract that he spent ten minutes coughing up the caviar that he had just half-swallowed as he heard the news. He then spent weeks suffering from convulsions that became so severe that they caused structural changes to his silvery follicles. For weeks, he had terrible hair problems.

Levels of astonishment were unparalleled as the news ricocheted around the world's most luxurious holiday resorts that Svetlana had turned aside a multi-million-dollar-a-year contract as the world's most acclaimed model to study Roman history at Bradford University and "to meet real people."

"Unfortunately," the stoic Paulo announced, repressing a gulp, "my faucets have deranged her."

Why else would any woman have left him? Only insanity could have caused this. Unable to face the faucets, he had them changed to sliver.

In Bradford, Svetlana met Dave Batley, a short, fat, bald plumber with a gift of the gab who was also fascinated by Roman history.

Soon the news blasted through Europe's most elite holiday spots that Svetlana was "dating a tub who mends tubs."

That news was galvanising for Paulo, as it was unassailable evidence that Svetlana's mental state had been impaired permanently by her head's crashing against his ex-faucets that had been pawned off to a dealer in New York at a price that had made the dealer's eyes shimmer like moonlight on water.

"I didn't acquire them," the dealer gloated at a Manhattan dinner party. "I snared them."

The famous faucets that had deranged the seductive Svetlana Hiptopski were now priceless. It was laughable for the great Paulo Bombasini that she could have left him for an obese plumber whose idea of fun was "gulping down of buckets of beer in a frozen cultural desert." Paulo's afflicted sense of justice became emboldened when silver-haired Diamante Briatore declared: "To leave a man like you, she must be the craziest cow on Earth."

It was the truest thing that Paulo had ever heard.

But Svetlana was fascinated by Dave and vice versa. They were inseparable. Conversation flowed between them like a high-tension wire: one comment and the thing would gyrate in both directions for hours. Svetlana had never laughed so much. Nor had she ever felt such fascination as Dave peeled off constant fascinating facts about he who had conquered the Galls. Dave was oblivious of his intelligence; until meeting Svetlana, beautiful women had assumed he had leprosy. His working-class modesty didn't allow him to take his friends' opinions about his intellect seriously.

Then disaster returned. Svetlana slipped, cracking her head against the plumbing in Dave's bathroom: what Dave's plumbing lacked in aesthetic brilliance was overcompensated for by technical panache. Svetlana's head had had plenty to aim at. It couldn't fail to miss the engine-room elaboration.

When she came to, she screamed: A short, fat, bald creature, with plump jowls, was above her; she yelped: "Where is my bag!"

Prior to her first fall, every time she had woken, her first thought had been the whereabouts of her favorite bag. This concern had given her a reputation for "sensitivity."

"My bag!" she howled. "And what are you doing with me? What is this place?"

"It's my bathroom," Dave said.

She pushed him aside with the fraught impatience that only horror induces; on seeing her bag, she was even more shocked: it was a backpack. After having been stopped in her tracks by this bewildering sight, she plundered its contents in pursuit of her cell phone. She rang Diamante.

"Diamante, darling," she yelped, "rescue me."

Diamante rose sharply from his easy chair. Only an extreme crisis could have got him to rise so rapidly from his position under Nice's promenade before the sedate waters of the world's most famous sea.

"Of course, darling," he said, ripping off his silver-white-framed sunglasses with a haste that only the most serious of matters can induce.

The frames matched his silver follicles perfectly.

"But, darling," he added. "Where are you?"

"I'm," she gulped, "in a place that's indescribable."

"Is it Bradford?"

Svetlana fled to a window. A sign above a kebab shop, containing the word "Bradford," was just visible through a dreary, grey curtain of precipitation.

"Oh God," she belched. "I'm in Bradford!"

"Keep calm, darling," Diamante insisted. "Find out the address. I'll send around a taxi. Tell the driver to take you to the nearest five-star hotel. Ring me when you get there. I'll arrange payment."

"Oh, darling, thank you."

She spun, demanding: "What's the address?"

"You don't know?" Dave replied.

"What is your address?"

She stomped on the weather-beaten carpet.

"15 Pratsworth Road," Dave said.

"Diamante: it's 15 Pratsworth Road."

Svetlana then spent a "shocking ten minutes" in a small "enclosure" with a creature whose blubber wobbled when it moved. Svetlana believed that she had never been in the same room with anyone who had blubber—and who was bald. It was terrifying. She stood between it and the sofa. It was unimaginable that she could have been in a dingy place with a beast whose corpulence shivered when it moved; she almost dry-retched.

Her hands frantically searched for the doorknob when the taxi driver—a private chauffeur—rang the bell.

"Quick!" she said. "The nearest five-star hotel. What is it?"

"The Sheraton in Birmingham."

"Birmingham has got five-star hotels?!"

She rang Diamante who had been waiting hysterically on his easy chair. The tension had even caused sweat to defeat his favorite deodorant.

"Darling, darling," he said, feigning a deep calmness that indicated his steely professionalism in a crisis, "stop worrying. The hotel will pay the driver. They'll look after you. I'll arrange everything. I'll get you on a private jet to Monaco tomorrow."

"Oh, Diamante, you're an angel."

"Oh, Baby, you know it's nothing."

Svetlana's vocabulary had regained its pre-Dave "sensitivity." During her time with Dave, her speech became so unaffected that she didn't even say "awesome." During her catwalk phase, "awesome" had constantly been employed by her in press interviews to describe the "brilliance" of those that she had had "the great fortune to have worked with."

"Simply awesome," had slipped out when she had been particularly moved by the thrill of having worked with "geniuses" like Exquisatore Extraordinaire or the pony-tailed paparazzi Xavier L'Charme who could "turn concrete to diamonds by pressing a button."

Dave spent weeks being consoled by his mates.

"This was," he said, "my York United versus Man U." York United's greatest moment had been an FA Cup victory over Manchester United at Old Trafford.

"But who knows," he added. "Even Crystal Palace got back into the Premier League."

"That's the spirit, son," one of his mates said.

In Monaco, surrounded by the spiritually fulfilling beauty of unlimited wealth, Svetlana flew into Diamante's arms. Her heart pumped with relief.

"Oh, Diamante," she said, "I can't believe it. I was in Bradford! How's Paulo?"

Diamante couldn't hide his measured concern. He deliberately couldn't hide it.

"Darling, what is it?" she cried. "Darling" had been used more by her in the previous twenty-four hours than in the previous three months.

"Let's have a drink," Diamante replied, a common phrase when horrifying news was to be imparted.

When Svetlana discovered that Paulo was now dating the sly, vindictive Claudia Cash-Bonkerssen, her archenemy on the catwalks, she gasped, just managing to stop the hors d'oeuvre in her mouth from blocking her throat.

"I'm dreadfully sorry," Diamante said.

Appropriate Concern was in his job description. The ability to feign compassion was fundamental; every time one of his models made a romantic decision, it was invariably a stupid selection. He had had plenty of opportunities to refine his art. In most cases, he had accurately predicted disaster, hence had had adequate time to practice his calculated shock in front of his bathroom mirror. This also gave him another excuse to admire himself.

Claudia Cash-Bonkerssen had been a cauldron of envy, unable to accept that she was merely number two "in the eyes of the world"—that the sleek, graceful Svetlana Hiptopski was her nemesis, in the opinion of the press and her fellow professionals.

During Svetlana's brief, intense flurry with Dave Batley, Julius Caesar, and the Roman Republic, Claudia and Paulo had formed a mutual pack of revenge against the "arrogant" Svetlana. The more arrogant someone is, the more they accuse others of this ailment. Not even the chauffeur used this expression to describe Svetlana's finicky behavior; he expected it, happy to acknowledge his "position in the pecking order." But being paid a lot for doing nothing stabilises one's perception.

Snouts were pointed skyward with frank bitterness one sultry day in Milan, when Svetlana and Claudia exhibited Exquisatore Extraordinaire's latest additions to pointless attire. Despite the chilly atmosphere in the thirty-five-degree heat, the warring pair gritted their teeth to expose "to the world" pineapple hats and giant-red-pepper dresses, Exquisatore having had the wilting creativity of having connected fabric with fruit. Amid such "brilliance," neither Svetlana nor Claudia wanted to be one who would crack and be accused of "small-mindedness." Both courageously rose above the trivial to present the genius of a man who said: "Nails could have been bared at any moment. But they both rose brilliantly above personal differences to demonstrate their flair in the face of absurdity—sorry, I mean adversity."

It had been trying for everyone, especially for Claudia who threw down a newspaper when the press reported that she been "edged ever so slightly by Svetlana Hiptopski in Milan."

It had been trying, but everyone, except Claudia, was delighted that Svetlana had "returned to her senses."

Then Svetlana slipped again—on a catwalk in Paris. Years later, Claudia admitted that the moisturizer that she had strategically located near the catwalk's entrance, during a break in proceedings, had done the job.

Given that she admitted guilt without a police investigation, she only got two months for manslaughter.

"In a sense," she said, "it was my Rubicon."

# THE ARSENALE

**Nancy Caronia**

I gazed on Vito's scars and watched how they danced in the sunlight and rippled as he emerged from the sea. I imagined I could know him from the marks on his body. I drank from his nakedness in the hopes of understanding my scars better. His were visible for the world to see. I believed mine left no discernible trace.

For the two and one half months I lived on the island of Capri, I ran to the Arsenale each morning so Vito and I could spend time alone. My morning ritual began with Tai Chi and breakfast at my *pensione*. *Una camomilla, per favore. Un panino formaggio.* The *pensione* owner believed I was dangerous with my wooden sword stabbing the sun as it rose. His wife found it strange that I did not drink *caffé*, not even *caffé americano. Per me, caffeina é male*, I explained in my rudimentary Italian each morning how my body shook if I drank even a cola. She shook her head and brought me a pot of tea that she thought would serve me better in the evening than first thing in the morning.

After breakfast, I packed my writing notebook and my swimsuit before walking quickly through the narrow alleys, jumping onto the cement path of the Via Krupp, smelling the bougainvillea and jasmine, plucking a honeysuckle blossom to suck the juice, touching the cacti, examining a green lizard or two, and checking to see how far the sun had already traveled that morning. I threw myself onto the rock path forged from the feet of sun worshippers going back 2,000 years. I stared at the sea to see if it was a good day for swimming and always, always, I searched for Vito.

The first time I saw Vito, he appeared to me as a real-life Poseidon standing at the edge of the sea, the cave of the Arsenale, a 2,000-year-old Roman naval fortress, at his back. His weathered, compact, and nude body drank in sunbeams. His hair was shoulder-length and sun-bleached, a scruffy beard covered his ruddy face, and he had scars along his arms, legs, back, and cheeks. Although I imagine him sometimes with a trident in his right hand, he was not holding one that day or any of the subsequent days I was in his company. At that time, Vito was 50 years old and proud he didn't look a day over 40. He exercised every morning, running in place, doing sit-ups, and swimming in the sea. The only way of knowing his age was by close observation of the gray making its first appearance in his beard and the crow's feet forming around his eyes. He was my cicerone, loving Capri more than any of the natives of the island. Born in Bari, a small town on the east side of the Italian mainland along the Adriatic Sea, he arrived in Capri at 20 years of age and simply stayed. There was an irony to his presence on the island. He resembled the figure of *Man* in Dieffenbach's paintings that hung in Capri's Carthusian monastery. These religious paintings depict man's struggle with god and nature. I wondered how Dieffenbach felt Vito's presence fifty years before Vito was even born, since the likeness was not simply reminiscent, but exact. Dieffenbach's work only enhanced my sense that Vito was a god.

It was common knowledge among Vito's friends that Vito, though he pretended not to, lived in a smaller cave next to the Arsenale. The Caprese thought he was intellectually slow, but he seemed to like his isolation from the townspeople, except for his chosen compatriots. The cave itself was sparsely furnished with different items carried down the rocky path by the *ragazzi pigri* or "*lazy boys*" as Vito and his friends—Peppino, Antonio, Roberto, Pasquale from Naples, and Teó, a retired Belgian—called themselves. Roberto was the youngest at 38 and Antonio, at 66, was the oldest. There was also a heavy metal door that the *lazy boys* had somehow fit into the mouth of the cave. It was locked each evening to keep thieves from stealing Vito's and the other men's items.

As my infatuation with Vito's life grew, I teased him that I might stay on Capri and move into the cave. At first, he shrugged his shoulders and gestured that he didn't think I would be able to survive the nights. As the weeks wore on, I kept up my chant of *I'm moving in*, and he changed his tone and said, in a dialect I didn't understand, but could comprehend: *it wouldn't be that difficult because you wouldn't need much money to live.*

I wanted to believe him. I wanted to believe my feelings for Vito were genuine. Each morning, as I jumped from rock to rock drinking in the beauty of the azure and emerald sea, I noticed the shapes of the cotton ball clouds along the horizon, and held my breath until I spotted him. Vito sat meditating on a rock in the early morning hours, staring out at the Faraglioni, the pyramid-shaped rock formations that sprang from the middle of the Tyrrhenian Sea. He told me those rocks gave him internal strength. If I caught him in the middle of his meditation, I approached quietly, not wanting to disturb his solitude, checking to make sure that I was the first person there besides Vito. He'd turn towards me, knowing I was there before he saw me, and our morning ritual began.

*Ciao, Nancy.*

*Ciao, Vito.*

We'd smile tentatively, slowly, inquiringly, and the silence of the day would fall around us. The morning was filled with these silences. He'd jump up from the rock he sat on, stretch his naked body to the sun, and run back to the cave to grab cushions for us to lie on. We stared at the sea, at the horizon, at the rocks, at the stray cats that lived with Vito in the Arsenale, anything but each other. Every so often, Vito would click his tongue to the roof of his mouth. I'd turn to him and open my mouth to speak, but no words came. We'd look deeply at each other for a moment and then one of us would exhale and look away.

I sunbathed topless at the Arsenale, losing my American self-consciousness about the corporal self. One morning, I made the decision to sunbathe nude. I was alone with Vito in the morning. I trusted him. I was testing him. I was testing me.

I didn't trust the rest of the lazy boys in this way. I craved an even, no-line tan, but the lazy boys encouraged me to sunbathe nude and I knew their intentions were purely voyeuristic. I couldn't do it. They made me uncomfortable; I'd roll my eyes at them, cast my eyes downward, and utter, *No*. End of discussion. My sense that they were voyeurs caught up with them when I discovered a hidden video camera in the cave. It was used for the purpose of taking videos of any unsuspecting women tourists that the lazy boys befriended. One day, I heard the camera whir above the sounds of the waves outside and turned to see a red light staring at my crotch. I changed into my swimsuit out of camera range, went to the sea, and sat with my legs dangling over the edge of the rocks. I stared at the horizon, wondering what I was going to say to them. The lazy boys gathered in conference above me. Pepino, Roberto, and Antonio huddled together. Vito sat away from them, listening and looking guilty. Roberto, the best speaker of English, finally approached me. Before he could utter a word, I surprised myself and him by spitting out: *If I ever see that camera again, Roberto, I'll smash it on the rocks.*

He looked skeptical, but cautious. *What do you mean, Nancy?*

*I know about the camera, Roberto, and I don't want to see it again.*

*But, Nancy, in January, when there are not a lot of women, we look at the videos that Pepino takes over the summer.* Roberto thought he'd given me a worthy explanation and smiled.

*Whoa! You have a collection?*

*Si,* his smile began to fade.

*Well, you can't have my naked butt on video. I don't want to see it again or, I swear, Roberto, I will smash Pepino's precious video camera on a rock and no one will ever use it again. Capisci?*

He understood. Pepino, too, understood and didn't like that they were letting a young woman have her way. Vito looked relieved that I hadn't hit anyone. And me? I sat there shaking, amazed that I'd actually opened my mouth and told them off. Some women might have allowed the lazy boys to tape them; they might have even performed for them, understanding how slow and lonely the winter can be on Capri. Others might have been outraged and left, but these men had become my friends, or so I felt them as my friends in spite of their flirtations and encouragement to sunbathe nude. The betrayal lay in the idea that, ultimately, they saw me as a sexual object worth fooling. I was confused because I wanted, or I thought I wanted, Vito to see me as sexually alluring. There

I was, 32 years old and feeling like a schoolgirl. I was a teenager with Vito, something I missed out on growing up on Long Island. A place I ran from as soon as I thought I could safely get away. An island whose beauty I never noticed, only felt my breath stolen from me at every attempt to assert who I was.

That first time I lay naked, Vito was napping. My body tingled with the sensation of danger. When Vito awakened, I pretended to doze off, to make believe nothing had changed, but I knew in my heart I had offered something that I wasn't sure I wanted to be received. Too many times in my youth, my body was taken without permission, and now I was freely offering something I still wasn't positive I wanted to give.

I felt Vito's gaze that morning, and then I heard him sigh and turn away. I turned to him and watched his back breathing. I examined closely the twining scar that ran along his side to the top of his buttock. I ran my fingertips over it without touching Vito's skin. I felt the shape of that scar, through the distance, how deep it ran and wanted to crawl inside it.

This morning, as with most every morning, the lazy boys' arrival broke the spell Vito and I were under. We two became hyper-animated. I spoke in my broken Italian to the other men, pointing my conversation towards Antonio, the oldest of the bunch. Vito talked non-stop in dialect to everyone and no one, cursing up a storm. As the mornings slid lazily into afternoons, the change was noted in the position of the sun and the shadows on the rocks. After a lunch of tuna, fresh tomato, and basil sandwiches, made with care by Pasquale, like kindergarten children, we napped. Vito and I rested our legs on the rocks and observed the clouds as we'd drift in and out of sleep, telling each other what we saw: *Santa Claus. A bunny. Lenin—not John, the Beatle, but the Russian revolutionary.* The other men watched our dance in fascination and with a bit of envy. When they attempted to discover what was going on between us, Vito shut down conversation with a look or his "I am an honorable man" speech.

About a week after I sunbathed nude, but two weeks before I was to leave the island, I arrived late and found all the men gathered near the water, speaking rapidly in dialect. An event was taking place, but I wasn't in on it. For the first time since my arrival, they barely took in my presence. Roberto was laughing with Antonio. Teó, Pasquale, Pepino, Renato, and others I didn't know, were gathered like women waiting to help a friend through childbirth.

Suddenly, Vito bounded forward over the rocks. He was wearing a short lime-green and black spandex set of trunks and carried a small knife. With a goofy-eyed grin, he yelled *ciao, Nancy*, and dove into the sea. The men clapped their hands, their mouths open in delight. Vito emerged about 100-feet out and then disappeared. He came up for air and dove a few times until Pepino screamed, *Ecco lo! Ecco lo!* The men were shouting to each other, slapping each other on the back. *What's going on?* I yelled, but no one paid attention. I noticed, as Vito emerged from the sea, he had something in his hands because the knife was in his mouth. He looked like an underwater Tarzan.

I sat near the ladder made especially by these men to help tourists and older people in and out of the water. The natives rarely used it, but Vito surprised me by climbing up it. He'd placed an octopus on his head like a hat. Two of the tentacles were above his lips like a handlebar mustache. I screamed: *oh god, that's disgusting!* Vito put his face close to mine and garbled nonsensically. Roberto turned towards me with a scowl: *It's beautiful! Men must eat, no?* I screamed again, trying to move away from Vito while he danced a wild tarantula, the octopus on his head still, and the men singing along. When the dance was done, he threw the octopus on the rocks. He smashed it again and again, a white foam spewing from the grey blob. I shouted: *you're hurting it.* Roberto turned to me: *Nancy, it's already dead. Vito killed it in the ocean with the knife.* Vito looked at me and said in English: *it's to make the meat tender.* All the men took their turn smashing it onto the rocks. It was the first time I felt like an invader to the lazy boys' summer rituals.

Later that day, Vito cooked the octopus over the fireplace in the smallest of the caves that the men had outfitted as a kitchen. The stray cats hovered nearby, hoping to get some of the treat. He stated, casually, in Italian, not dialect, that if I wanted to stay for supper, I could. His look was hopeful. All the men became silent, waiting for my reply. I was ungracious and shook my head no. His face registered disappointment.

The day of the hunter was the first time I recognized how lonely Vito was. I had been focused only on my desire. That afternoon, I lay near the sea and looked back at Vito, who sat at a table by his cave. He wore a blue t-shirt and had a dirty towel wrapped around his torso. The men had all scattered—they had families and jobs to return to. This occurrence was normal: I stayed with Vito until sunset. Vito had no family and I was a tourist. That late afternoon, I noticed as his arms hung at his sides and his head was bent forward to his chest, how fragile he was. I knew in that moment I had the power to hurt him. I recognized that he didn't have anything figured out any more than I did. I wanted to be more careful, but didn't know how. I wanted the fantasy not the reality, but the reality had come crashing in anyway.

I must have fallen asleep because, when I woke up, the sun was low on the horizon, and Vito was standing above me. He stared for a long time before he spit out: *I am not strónzo*. I didn't know the exact meaning of the word, but I knew it had to do with me acting one way, but wanting another. I answered him with silence. He said: *I am a man. Lo so*, I answered. *Lo so, Vito*.

He bounded back to his home and entered the cave. He emerged fully clothed. I shifted to a flat rock that fit my body perfectly and waited for Vito to finish his metamorphosis from Poseidon, the god of the sea, to Vito, the island's homeless eccentric. While I waited, I watched the night fishermen light their lamps and head out for the open sea. Fall arrived on Capri in the sunsets. Pink and orange streaks through clouds outlined in a baby blue.

Vito walked slowly from the cave in his white pants and white and red stripped button-down cotton shirt, his sneakers and socks in one hand. At the end of this day, like each day, we fell back into our silence, the quiet intimacy of people who know one another. He stood staring at the sea. Finally, he looked at me: *Andiamo*. Together, as always, we walked to the civilization of the small town where he dropped me off close to, but not at, my *pensione*.

Normally, once we arrived on the Via Krupp, Vito became talkative. It was as if that much movement on our parts, along with the setting of the sun, needed words to fill the empty spaces and lengthening shadows. He told me the names of the plants, where the Naples boys hid their drug needles and, sometimes, my favorite times, he sang to me. He imitated Frank Sinatra or Dean Martin perfectly, but mostly he sang Neapolitan love songs that I didn't understand, but knew deep in my cell structure.

That early evening, the evening when I rejected Vito's dinner invitation, we stopped halfway up the Via Krupp and waited for the sunset to completely hide itself behind Monte Solaro. The air was beginning to chill in this late fall evening and our faces were in shadow when Vito whispered under his breath. I took a step towards him, the closest we'd ever been, asking him to repeat what he'd said. Our cheeks brushed close without touching, our lips exhaled breath onto each other's ears. My heart beat fast as I smelled the salt of the sea on him; he really was a sea creature, not human. His eyes penetrated mine in the darkness and then he took a step away, tilted his head, and said nothing. We stood like that for a minute, and he broke the silence by shaking his head as if to say: *Nothing, I didn't say anything.* He dug his hands deep into his pockets as he motioned with his shoulder for me to follow. We walked silently the rest of the way.

When we arrived near my pensíone, he took a step towards me, his hands still in his pockets. *Ciao, Nancy.*

*Ciao, Vito. Ci vediamo.*

*Si, Nancy. A domaini.*

We parted for the evening as we always had, as if day and night put us on opposite ends of the world, without another word.

Vito is past seventy now, and I have heard from a friend that his memory is not so good and his health is failing him. He still lives in the cave on a precipice overlooking the sea. I want to remember his way with the Dean Martin songbook and his jokes I never understood. I want to remember the man who taught me the power of meditation. I want to remember the only man on Capri who would save tourists when they tried to swim in the sea during a storm. Most especially, I want to remember Vito as the man who refused to take advantage of a not so young woman when she behaved like the young girl she still believed she was.

# APOGEE

**Thomas Piekarski**

In the ivory hours
of teentsy-weentsy mornings
they'd break the sound barrier
with huge ka-booms,
those jets taking off from Mather
and McClellan Air Force bases.

The vapor trails they left
in the brilliant blue sky
extended even beyond
heaven's horizon.

It was the apogee
of Cold War reconnaissance
hysteria that gripped
both sides as they amassed
monstrous nuclear arsenals
in a square world.

# THE BAD FATHER

**Tim Conley**

As you may have yourself discovered, just when the shops are closing is a terrible time in which to find a gift for a party later that evening, and this was the quandary in which Clive found himself less than an hour before he was due at his ex-wife's house. Snow was teasing the sky and effected a certain panic among the cars below, which made finding a place to park that much more of a job. A side street was tried after another side street, and after that a narrower side street, Clive muttering the unheard-of street names as curses, looking at signs, trying to look around or through obstacles. The lights of shops went out one after another.

Having parked far from those dimming commercial lights, Clive jogged the way a man who does not typically exercise in this way jogs through the side streets, turning here and there. He found a candy store with those nice lemon drops, a stationer's shop with fancy pens, a few places that might have sold something to the purpose, all closed. He had no idea what he was looking for beyond the general concept of buying a gift, and he was breathing heavily when he stopped at a shop window he almost didn't spot, peered in, tried to figure out whether the place was still open.

The door pushed open, but the place was dank and dark. Clive gradually made out various crowded and cobwebbed shelves and an antique cash register. Empty birdcages. Lamps, candlesticks, a row of eye-droppers. Coiled springs nestled in boxes with speckled handkerchiefs. A sextant leaning against a microscope. Jars of marbles and towers of spools. Expressionless figurines in uncertain poses. Bookends shaped like owls. A xylophone or something very like one.

The owner, if that's who it was, slowly shuffled into view from behind a curtained doorway. It might have been a man or a woman, but for that matter it might have been an animated pile of papers and dust, for so it looked. The tendered smile was made of a thousand interwoven facial creases; the voice that offered assistance rattled deep within.

Still looking round at the unpromising bric-a-brac all about him, Clive hurriedly explained the need for a suitable present for his daughter, something unique and needed immediately. "It is her tenth birthday. She is an unusual girl. She likes unusual things." As he was speaking, his gaze slipped through a pile of beaten boxes on a high shelf. He reached up to move the boxes aside and pulled down the dull red object there. It was not a ball, as he had first thought, but a polyhedron, whose vertices were puckered with dials, and its faces alternately engraved with markings and punctured with delicate little holes. Porcelain maybe, but very old. Clive held up the ball in vain hopes of seeing it in a better light, and then applied his eye to one of the holes. Flakes and tiny sticks of shifting colors coalesced into a moving shape, then into another, and another, as he could not help turning the object in his hands. Was that a woman dancing? No, now it was two men fencing, and now a proud horse leaping until it became a massive shining bird, which flew high until it burst into flame.

"What is this?" The question, he realized as he asked it, didn't matter.

"If it has a proper name," the proprietor answered with a chuckle akin to a snake's cough, "I have forgotten it. We might satisfactorily call it an amusement. It is unique, and the story goes that the master who devised this original amusement, at the behest of a potentate's child, died after its completion. Yet its history is even more singular than that."

"Great," said Clive.

"It is said that the young heir in question disappeared not very long after the amusement was given to him. It is said that he played with it for days, turning it round and round, twisting the dials, unlocking its abilities and its secrets. Nothing but it could hold his attention: he took it with him to his bed at night and began his mornings with it in his hands. But one day the servants found the amusement sitting unattended on the floor of the heir's bedchamber, and the young heir was nowhere to be found. There was speculation that the amusement had swallowed the young heir's soul."

"Sounds perfect," said Clive. He had missed—had actually forgotten—last year's birthday. Not this year.

"But beware," the gnarled face continued, and a bony finger rose before it, "if it is exposed to the light of a full moon: for these apertures will take in that luminescence and awaken a mystery best left dormant within the device. Flout it at all other times, in any weather, but on the night of a full moon, wrap it in some thick cloth, store it in shadow, keep it far from the full moon's light."

"Got it," said Clive. The party was due to start in ten minutes, and it was going to take at least twice as long to get there, and he still had to get back to the car.

"We have called it an amusement, for the sake of convenience, and it is a very old and remarkable amusement, perhaps even an endlessly diverting amusement, but there are very specific conditions for how it may be given as a gift and how it is to be handled. No one else should play with it but the person to whom it is given. It is for her and her alone. Others who try to usurp it or possess it without permission may find it harmful. The amusement belongs only to whom it is given, and the amusement will resent the presumptions of others."

"Great," said Clive.

"Above all, there is one most important prohibition. The child may look through any of the apertures and delight at the visions she finds within, but not this aperture," and the bony finger identified the one in question, which looked no different at all from the others, "never this one. There are great dangers in this one."

"Great," said Clive.

"There are those who believe that play is inextricably bound up with danger, and there are those who believe this is as it should be. Of such things have I no judgment. Yet even such an ancient fool as I readily observe that some hazards can never be properly called part of play, even if play may lead one towards them."

"Great," said Clive. "How much?"

The proprietor did not seem to understand the question.

"How much do you want for it?"

"Oh," came the reply, "thirty-six fifty-five."

Then Clive was out into the snow, now in earnest and joined by wind, reckoning its adverse effect on his estimated time of arrival.

Clutching the hastily wrapped amusement under his arm, he tried to remember whether this next corner was a left or a right. His ex-wife would have nothing so unique, nothing with such rich history to it, the magical bauble that would belong to her and to her alone, but that last corner did look familiar. He retraced his steps, already quickly filling in behind him, and then retraced those other steps. There was the shop with the cheap lemon drops. That was encouraging. He took another right. A young couple, arm in arm, passed him, but their intimate laughter stopped him from asking the name of the street. He took another left. Then another.

Like a beacon, a blue light ahead shone out between the blowing streaks of white. Clive thought suddenly and stupidly of the fairy who transforms Pinocchio, and it may have been this sudden and stupid thought that prevented him from breaking into a sprint, to see the light for what it was and try to get to the truck before it towed his car out of the private lot and away, away. But it was going away by the time he was running, and he shouted as he ran, and tried to bang his arm against the side of the truck, but could not even see the driver or be sure that he was being heard. He shouted again and struck again, but the truck dragging his defeated car was away, well away.

It had not been just his arm that had struck the truck. The gift lay irreparably in pieces in the deepening snow, the torn wrapping flapping about. His eyes itched, or perhaps just the one eye, the eye that had seen the dancing woman and the duelists and the leaping horse and the shining bird and the fireball. His hands were empty and it was late.

He went to a bar, which he had no difficulty finding, and got very drunk, very nearly carelessly drunk.

Late the next day he telephoned his ex-wife and made apologies and excuses, but his daughter, the unusual girl of ten, never spoke to him again.

Has this ever happened to you?

# A DASH IN LAGOS

Laine Strutton

I arrived in Nigeria with nothing more than an out-of-date guidebook, my backpack, and a chip on my shoulder. I was halfway through my PhD and had decided that Nigeria was politically fascinating, important to the global economy, and understudied. All my university colleagues advised me to pick an easier country, a safer country, and the more they tried to dissuade me, the more committed I became to writing a dissertation on the oil violence in the Niger Delta. The conflict has pitted government forces against militants demanding oil revenues and stealing from pipelines, often with local community members caught in the middle. Oil spills have destroyed local fishing and farming practices. The average Niger Deltan is actually poorer than they were at national independence in 1960. I wanted to write about it.

After several months of grueling field research there, in which I had interviewed militants in the swamp, waded through toxic rivers, and shared a canoe with crocodile, I needed some time off in the capital. I flew to Lagos because I wanted just a single day without the challenges of life in rural communities. I thought that if I left the Delta, I might enjoy a few hours in which I didn't have to obsess over my personal safety and health or carefully navigate the complexity of Nigerian culture. I just wanted a day at the beach, and I had heard of just the one.

During my respite, I was staying with a Lebanese friend in his posh gated home in the most upscale area of Lagos, Victoria Island. The immense wealth inequality in the country means that one can build a gated mansion and, yet, there will still be entrepreneurial street-side vendors and motorcycle taxis cruising for customers right outside that gate. Indeed, I walked out of my host's compound and was able to immediately hop on the back of an *okada* motorcycle taxi. After naming the fashionably private beach that I wanted to go to, my driver deftly navigated the freeways and bridges connecting the many islands of the chaotic city. During the ride, I looked out over the millions of residents who had built shanty towns in the water on floating mounds of trash and who commuted via barges made of reeds. I was certain that I was probably going to be the first person to ever arrive to the private beach wearing an ill-fitting helmet while straddling the back of an *okada*, the same working-class form of transport slum residents often take.

When we arrived at the small dirt road leading to the beach, I felt the motorcycle slow, and I looked ahead to see that rain the night before had inundated the pathway. A small lake had formed, actually erasing the road altogether. Flooding is a perpetual problem in Nigeria, and during my time there, I counted myself lucky to never have had to evacuate like so many of my Nigerian friends had. I asked the driver about another entrance and was disappointed when he said there wasn't one because of the large and formidable fence along the beach. As a testament to both my commitment to relaxation, and my ability to ignore my better judgment when sand and surf is involved, I suggested the name of a slightly seedier, but still somewhat reputable, beach nearby. It was on the way back toward Victoria Island anyway, so my driver didn't even charge me extra for the change in itinerary. I thought that was some good fortune on my part.

Several minutes later, I felt my driver's body tense as we turned a corner toward the second-choice beach. He had spotted a dozen menacing-looking *area boys* in front of us. *Area boys* are urban gangs of unemployed men that harass, steal, extort, and sell drugs, and they have a fierce reputation for having no limits on their use of violence. As they had with us that day, they commonly set up their own impromptu roadblocks and force motorists to pay a *dash*, or bribe, to pass. They have merited their malevolent reputation by consistently following through with their threats against those who don't or can't pay. Alarming to me, who had survived in Nigeria by appealing to a sense of compromise during worrisome encounters, many had told me that *area boys* simply can't be reasoned with. As we drove in closer, I felt that instinctual tightening in my belly that we all get in times of danger.

When my driver hesitantly pulled up to their makeshift roadblock made of trash, wood, and palm leaves, the *area boys* immediately began using 2x4s to fiercely beat on the front of the motorcycle. They were screaming in Pidgin English, "Pay us 500 naira for pass! Pay us now for pass!" Although my driver probably did not share this thought, I was just grateful that the wooden planks were coming down on the motorcycle and not on us.

As a foreign traveler, I am faced with a special dilemma, both ethical and pragmatic. First, I do not want my presence to be funding extortionist behavior in foreign countries. By paying this bribe, I would be contributing to this criminal activity. I am very proud of the fact that I spent a year in one of the most corrupt countries on earth without paying a *dash*. My second dilemma was that a Nigerian riding an *okada* typically doesn't carry around more than a few dollars on them, which is all the *area boys* expect to get from an individual. However, these men knew that I probably had more than that on me since I am not Nigerian. I suspected that the moment I took my money pouch out to pay them the 500 naira, slightly more than just $3, they would just take my cell phone and all my money. I would be stranded, as I needed that naira to get home and to the airport the next day. My driver was so anxious he didn't speak, yet I was relatively calm, so I decided that I was in the best position to handle the situation.

I put on a jovial grin, batted my eyelashes a few times, and said in the most casual and non-confrontational voice I could, "Sirs, could I just pay on my way out from the beach? That would be more convenient for me. Is that possible?" Unsurprisingly, the *area boys* rejected this idea and yelled to my face that my offer was "no good!" Realizing that I was certainly not going to out-power them, I brainstormed new tactics. I picked out the man who seemed the oldest, and he was also the tallest, and pegged him for the leader. Relying on a conversation I had had often while serving as a secondary school teacher in the Peace Corps in Mozambique years earlier, I smiled at him, specifically, and said that I was just a poor teacher and that I couldn't afford to pay them. I asked him in all seriousness, "Do you offer a teacher discount for paying dash, in appreciation for all the hard work I have done educating African youth?"

This tallest one stared at me, his jaw fell slightly ajar, and he stammered, "No." He was clearly perplexed by my friendly response to their threats, and even more so by my ridiculous request for a teacher discount on this robbery. They all must have been wondering, *who is this strange white woman? Doesn't she know who we are?* After a pause, but with far less aggression than before, he continued to ask for 500 naira while the other *area boys* curiously watched behind him.

Understanding that there was only one other thing I had besides money to offer, I then made my ultimate bid. I asked him what his name was, which was Ahmed, and introduced myself by shaking his hand. I confidently said, "Ahmed, you are clearly an intelligent man. How about a trade? Instead of paying you, I offer you a free English lesson. I am an expert teacher and we can do any English lesson you want. Education is priceless, after all." Ahmed cocked his head to the side and responded slowly in pidgin, surprising me by saying, "Yeah, I want English lesson. Leave me to find a pen and a paper." I said I needed to go eat something, but that I would come back in an hour to give him his lesson. The other gang members looked on, dumbfounded, as I sent away the driver and hopped off the motorcycle to walk toward the ocean.

After I had eaten my spicy goat and rice for lunch, on the beach, I walked back to give Ahmed his lesson as promised (and they were blocking the only road out, so I didn't have a choice but to encounter them again anyway). While sitting on the dusty road, a hundred feet from his gang that was still operating its roadblock, we did a vocabulary-building lesson. We covered words like "bellicose" to describe the gang's inclination toward fighting and "deceitful" to describe the character of his *area boys* who lie to him. I quickly realized I should have done a better assessment of his language skills before choosing such advanced words; he held the pen like he was cutting open a watermelon and frequently mixed up his vowels when I said them aloud. I apologized for my bad lesson, since it was my fault, and he responded that he would rather ask questions about the United States anyway.

Ahmed wanted to know all about getting jobs in America. He eagerly inquired as to whether he had a chance of finding a job driving a taxi in New York. I responded that I didn't know, but he could try to find that sort of job in Lagos. He told me that there are so few jobs in the country that someone without a high school degree has no chance at all of being hired, unless they can pay a dash to the employer. Nepotism pervades hiring practices there, so I knew that what he was saying was largely true. It is nearly impossible to work one's way up the socioeconomic ladder in Nigeria, as my research had shown me.

Over the course of the next half-hour in our classroom of sorts, Ahmed told me about how much he had always wanted to go to school, but his parents could never afford it because there are ten children in his family. I asked him about going back to study, but he responded that now that he is 30, he is just too old. Without a job, he has no way of earning money to pay a bride price to get married, so he felt like he would never get to start his own family. Essentially, because he couldn't afford to go to high school, his entire life as a productive adult has been put on hold. I was surprised when he added that he hated his lifestyle, of being an *area boy*, but felt that he had no other choice. I told him that I heard what he was saying, but most of the 167 million people in Nigeria live in poverty, too, and they make ends meet without harming others. He agreed.

After this frank conversation about his life conditions, it was strange to think that my new student had been willing to violently beat my driver and me earlier and had probably done so many times to others. I never forgot for one moment that he was a criminal and deserved some form of punishment for the choices he had made yet, every minute I spoke with him, he seemed more and more like a very frustrated man with no options in life. His demeanor during our talk was almost dejected, as he cast his face downward and spoke into his lap. I learned an incredible amount from him about the traps of cyclical urban poverty. I finished the talk wondering not why there is so much stealing and violence in countries like Nigeria, but why there isn't even more. I do not doubt that he has engaged in deplorable acts and his life story does not excuse them, but my conversation with him still gave me pause. Urban poverty and criminality is complex, and it had often deceived me into viewing it as simpler than it truly is.

As the sun beat down on us, I told Ahmed that I needed to get home before dark. He sent one of his boys to flag me down another motorcycle. As I hopped on, this new driver was demonstrably agitated by the presence of the men, and I told him not to worry. Ahmed thanked me profusely for our talk and said that he thought I was his "best teacher in English." Not only did he not ask me for money, he offered to pay for my *okada* ride, which I politely declined. We shook hands. I tied up my long skirt and situated my purse on my back for the bumpy ride home. As we took off, I looked back to see that the *area boys* were waving at me and smiling.

Although I would like to attribute it to my silver tongue, I know that it was a combination of factors outside of my control, including extreme good fortune, which allowed that interaction to end on a positive note. I know that a Nigerian without any money would not have been as lucky as I was. I still haven't figured out how such a dangerous situation managed to turn out so well. However, I have figured out how a New Yorker can tell that she has become culturally acclimated to Nigeria. It becomes clear when she talks her way out of a shakedown by a street gang while riding on the back of a motorcycle.

# GESTURES

**Nick LaRocca**

To cover the killing from several years back, I had an ad hoc staff of one young woman from the local college out there in Belle Glade, Florida, a quiet thing named Maria Maciel, a mother, married, twenty-one, who knew her way around town. She spoke as little as anyone I'd ever met. From the moment I met her, I wanted to whisk her away on a golden carpet. I really did think there might be a book in the project, too.

I was married, while Maria was more vulnerable: rouged cheeks, Mexican with Chicano, a little like a geisha with her almond eyes. That week, up in Starke, they were putting to death a young man named Alfonso Armstrong, who had walked into a family-owned grocery store in town—a store that had thrived for fifty years—and shot the beloved white owner of the place, a genuinely nice guy named Jimmy Kline.

The whole community, black, white, Latin, Arab, had come out to turn in Alfonso. It was his own father who drove him to the police station three days after the murder.

Jimmy's place was called the Great Alabama-Florida Southern Grocery. They'd sold pickled sausage right beside bait and lures to fish the canals, right beside good steaks brought in each weekday morning, the only place in the area that carried quality meat—or you could get frozen hamburger just like at Winn Dixie, fatty stuff to grill out. A dude named Dontavian Jones kept a barbeque out back, cut out of a rusty oil tank salvaged from someone's backyard, and from 11:00 to 2:00 he pedaled delicious goat and pork butt pulled off the bone, served on a Pepperidge Farm bun from the store.

It was Dontavian who'd heard the ruckus and right away the gunshot, and crazily went running in through the back entrance, as though to help. On the mute video, when he came around the counter and saw Jimmy's body, he brought his hands to his ears and screamed. The gunman was fleeing, rushing out the door, stiff-arming past a man on the walkway who must have gasped, certain he was done for.

At the time, I still had my voice. I was losing it, but I still had my cadence, inflection, and diction in symphony, a luxury, a misfortune.

I got moving around out there, and it was an extraordinary place, with tall sugar cane on every sliver of open land I could find, vast fields of it as far as the eye could see. And trailers with laundry hanging on lines. And this barbed-wired lot cut into the cane where a man lived in a yellow school bus with an old fashioned satellite dish in the back corner and two pit bulls that came sprinting to bark at cars if there wasn't much traffic on 715, bark until their throats were torn up. And churches everywhere, wealthy, long established productions built like fortresses, and new affairs, squat one-room or two-room rectangles. I peeked in a few to watch the silent prayer.

Or out at the home of Jimmy's family, over on the lake in the nicest area of town, a sprawling, brick ranch on a long, wide slice of property that ran green and lush to the levee.

I spoke with Jimmy's son, who had just turned thirty. Their daughter wouldn't speak with me. Called me Dennis Boaz, after the Gary Gilmore shyster, said I was trying to profit, as was the *Post*, from their pain. And Leslie, Jimmy's wife, had a few things to say, and less space in which to say them as the son took over.

Leslie, I'd noticed, had aged well except in the face, which had wrinkled and turned leathery around bulging eyes and a razor-blade mouth. She was very slender and wore leather pants and a smart, matching jacket. It was good and cool out, February, after football season, and workers were burning sugar cane along 715. Far from the burn, there at the lake, I could smell soot in air.

Maria had come close. We were positioned, the four of us, on the front porch. They hadn't invited us in because the daughter remained inside, marking her territory. The son, James, had taken a seat at a little smoker's table and kept shuffling the ashtray. Leslie sat in front of the big window, eventually asking for the tray so that she could light up. Maria and I stood off by the porch steps.

From the cigarettes, a new habit after her husband's murder, a rasp had grown in Leslie's throat, same as me, and she noticed mine, asked whether I had a cold.

I explained, "Constant soreness. It's a good thing I write for a living."

She looked me up and down. "You're too young for the parts to stop working."

"He's *my* age," James put in.

"Older than that one." She pointed a Virginia Slim at Maria. "She's shy. You're too shy, young lady."

All Maria did was giggle. She hadn't spoken much to me—in fact, had only answered questions, and usually with a yes or no or some quick explanation, but in a lovely voice, with a middle pitch. My voice, back during my twenties, had been soothing, masculine, thick—tenor as a stout. But on my recordings, it is a rumbling tractor. And now, it is a chopped and mangled yowl, delirious. I can seem engulfed by my voice, captive to its lunatic crackle.

"She expected to grow old with my father," the son explained, as Leslie fell quiet. "They had a lovely life together, nice enough children, never mind my sister. But she was always terrified of that store's location. Right on Martin Luther King.

"Dad kept smart hours. You have your Dixie Fried, and you have the two law and tax people, so during the day, bars on the windows or not, it's quiet, looks like a poor neighborhood in another country. But at night? Terrible. Everyone goes inside except the shadows. There's no sense being out there. Dad kept daylight hours, but I remember Mom'd lose sleep over it, especially while she was raising us. He could'a hired someone, and Mom told him just that, but he said relationships with customers paid for the roof and food. Mom didn't let it be—"

"I said no each time," Leslie put in.

The son glared at her for interrupting. His monologue turned: "Dad had a shotgun—back behind the counter. But he handed over the money. The goddamned boy just shot him. That boy was a football player. He wasn't some dropout gangbanger. His voice wasn't a ruffian's. I play back his plea for mercy at sentencing, and yes, I do get angry. Bitter. I think maybe that's why my father handed over the money. Heard that clean voice and thought, 'This kid ain't gonna hurt me.' Who knows, anymore," James concluded. "What's the slant of your article?"

"We want to see whether healing has taken place. I assume it has."

Maria moved close enough now that her shoulder was touching mine. My heart leaped. But her proximity was from fear, for James had developed a good, solid scowl.

"My father was a martyr. He did great things for the Belle Glade. Was generous to a fault with those people. You want me to say what? That we've moved past the racial divide?"

"Would it have been better if his murderer had been white, James? I'm sorry, but it's my job to ask. You don't have to answer."

"Yes, sir, it would have been," James said without hesitation. "Maybe a white man, or maybe a crazy man, or maybe a man who didn't get the money. I don't know. Maybe some thug. Dammit, yes, it would have been better! Anyone but a civilized person, a normal person—listen to that kid talk! Dad'd pulled that shotgun if he'd felt the boy would have squeezed the damn trigger!"

"That kid was no bum," Leslie cut in. "Came from a solid family. The father is a religious man. But, remember, James, the grocery store accepted food stamps."

When I met her eyes, big and black and intelligent, she dropped her glance to the ground.

"Yes, it somehow would have been better," she whispered. Her voice shook. "I would prefer you not print what we just said."

I glanced inside. The daughter had come closer, was sitting on the couch before the window, a slim thing like her mother. She turned and studied me. Sure, her eyes grew harder, colder, fiercer as a the seconds passed, but at first, it was a quiet, soft countenance I confronted, as though she'd done a bad deed, had not been caught, and was touched by the guilt of so easily moving on. If she had spoken, in that moment, it might have been to forgive me, but all we had were our expressions, which we had not mastered.

*

On the drive back to Clewiston, where the sugar company has its headquarters and there are nice hotels and passable restaurants, the ash of burned cane fell like the soot of bodies, thick enough that here and there I had to turn on my windshield wipers. I marveled at the young, beautiful, silent Maria sitting beside me, with her round face and geisha eyes, and how she only once took her hands from her lap to gesture as we finally had a conversation, as though she had been trained to be as mild as the Virginia Slims Leslie burned.

For a while, we talked about my dying voice, which she described as "a chainsaw."

She told me, "I feel for you. You have kind eyes. You want the best for people. Your wife must care for you very much."

She clamped shut, so I coaxed other, less comfortable opinions out of her. She had not been in Belle Glade when the murder occurred. She'd been visiting Mexico. When I asked, "So you were seeing family there?" she nodded and added, "Sebastian."

"Is he your husband?"

"No. No, my husband is from here."

"Who is Sebastian?"

"A boy I loved."

"You were visiting him?"

"Yes."

"What happened to him, Maria? Why didn't you marry him?"

"Yes, he was murdered," she said, oddly, as though agreeing with me. "The Sicarios killed him for his father, as a. . .*vendetta*, I think is the word."

She dropped her eyes to her lap and played softly with her fingers. She wore a sweat suit. It was bone colored, a cloudy kind of cotton, made to look aged.

"I'm sorry."

I didn't speak for a bit, ran the wipers to clear the ash that was falling. "So you were in love with Sebastian?"

"Yes."

"And your husband now?"

She glanced out the window. We were in no man's land, with burning cane crackling off the road out my window and the Everglades, jagged and ferocious, out hers. "He is a hard worker. Thirty-seven. Owns a house."

"And you have a son together?"

"Yes."

Suddenly, she grew animated. "He does not let me do anything. From the college to home. I cannot work. I can't go out with friends. From the college to home with the baby! I took this job because this job is temporary, and even then, I had to beg him and sit on his lap." She choked down how detestable it was. "In work jeans. He never takes them off. They smell like chemicals. He never takes them off for dinner, even around the baby. I say, 'Those chemicals are no good for the baby.' But he never takes them off until he takes a shower, at the end of the night, and comes to bed and gets on top of me. I hate it! I hate him!"

She caught herself.

"Why don't you leave?"

She went on; all it took was a sympathetic glance. "After college. He does not know. I have to leave here. Miami, where he cannot find me. He would hurt me. He likes when I scream. I don't know if I can leave, like with Sicarios. Maybe he would find me. But I hate him. I can't look at him. He knows. He hates me. Screams at me and makes the baby scream. I will not leave, and that way, I will be like Sebastian.

"Maybe he will die young, from all the chemicals, or get sick and become too weak to hurt me. I don't want our son growing up with him. *He* is Sicarios. Sebastian never did nothin'. They murdered him for his father leaving their gang. I wish I knew him, still. He used to write the most lovely letters. I talked with him at night when I was a girl. I never got older from there. My husband says I'm beautiful because I look young. But I want to be seen as a woman, and if I was with Sebastian, I would have grown up—or if I just knew he was out there, I could go to him."

She was fighting back tears, though her face refused to tremble, and she turned inward, stoic. Up ahead, I saw signs for Clewiston, and further in the distance, the town rose out of the blankness and vastness of sugar cane, and I knew I'd better just take her to lunch on the paper's nickel and have her go back to the hotel to type up the transcripts, alone in the room with the voices of others.

\*

While she worked, I went down to the swimming pool and did some laps. The chlorine singed my throat. I moved back and forth, from the pool to the hot tub, trying to ignore the gleeful cries of two families on vacation together. I thought briefly of my own wife and children, but I put them out of my mind. I was a man suddenly without guilt, which made me a hollowed shell, and it was easy to know that Leslie hadn't loved Jimmy the way she should have—or, that was how Leslie felt. Surely, during arguments, she had said the words, "You're gonna get shot one day!" So when it happened, it was like a prayer she had come to believe would be answered. Or like Maria, who wanted to flashback to middle school, to late-night phone calls with Sebastian, when he would talk her to sleep with dreams of a better future. She believed he died because she did not open her heart to save him: had she confessed her love for him, he would have fled to Florida, and that gang would have sought their vendetta against someone else. Or that her baby boy has to hear and cannot speak, has to hear the cruel words of his father against his beautiful, young mother, words that flow from the ironic jealousy of comparison, Dad's gnarled working hands and intentional stink to Mom's silent beauty.

The jeans? To be disgusting. To revolt, then compel: true power.

"Crestor, twenty milligrams, for cholesterol. Lopressor, fifty milligrams, twice per day. Bayer, baby aspirin, the mild stuff, eighty-one milligrams for your heart. Let's keep those arteries pleasant."

I've learned to do by gesture. Here, with my doctor, a head nod. What's to say? He's the expert.

Most times, others don't want to hear your words, anyway. They want the beauty of their own speech, their own thoughts, which they've spent time with. They want you to listen. So a head nod suffices—that and a kind look in my eyes, as Maria pointed out and which I've learned to perfect because it and its several cousins make up my arsenal these days.

I speak only when I must.

"If you take Trish to her equestrian lesson, baby, I'll take Jason to Little League. We'll switch it up."

In response to this comment from my wife, I stuck out my bottom lip in thoughtful agreement. *What a nice change of pace.* For a moment, words seemed superior, but in the aftermath, I knew my silent agreement, garnished with gratefulness, was a more refined choice.

"Daddy, I love you."

I brought my eyes to meet Trish's lovely browns, the same color as her mother's. I am pleased this is my daughter, growing into her riding breeches.

"I should have made that play," Brian said.

This time, disagreement, but with compassion, understanding. He continued, "You saw it, Dad. It just got under my glove."

I gave a look that said, *You win some, you lose some.*

But what I wanted to say is, I dreamt of lights flickering down the road from Florida State Prison, Starke. The last moment of humanity was the condemned's mad dance, strapped to a chair, with a hood over his face to blind his eyes, to veil his contorted expressions. There was silence after his last words.

Because it wasn't the words. The hood was placed because no sane person would ever want to see his last look of reflection, witness his last voluntary silence, the horror in his eyes and all over his face, in the seconds after the words had been spoken, before the switch was flipped, when he knew and was telling you.

# A CONVERSATION WITH MATTHEW P. MAYO

*Lowestoft Chronicle*, October 2013

Matthew P. Mayo (Photography: Jennifer Smith-Mayo)

In the last six years, ever since the publication of his first novel in 2007, Matthew P. Mayo has authored more than two dozen books and dozens of short stories. His novel, *Tucker's Reckoning*, won the Western Writers of America's 2013 Spur Award for Best Western Novel, his short fiction has been a Spur finalist and a Western Fictioneers Peacemaker Award finalist, and his nonfiction books have garnered praise from numerous newspapers and magazines, including *The Boston Globe* and *Chicago Tribune*.

Recently, *Lowestoft Chronicle* managed to hunt down Mayo, who is currently traveling extensively across North America with his wife, in an Airstream trailer, to discuss his latest novel, *The Hunted*, as well as some of his other books and short stories.

**Lowestoft Chronicle (LC):** Your latest novel, *The Hunted*, is not only a truly great Western, but also a rivetingly gruesome horror story. There is a high body count of very grisly deaths, from people being scalped or gutted or burned alive. In fact, Chapter 34 is impossible to read on a full stomach. At one point in the novel you

The Hunted | Signet | 2013

write: "She didn't think it was possible to live through any more horrors and still remain in control of her mind. And then she knew that such a hope was foolish. Of course there were more horrible things to come, if only for the fact that there were still people alive for them to happen to…" What inspired *The Hunted*? Did you set out to write such a gory novel or did it simply happen that way as you began to write it?

**Matthew P. Mayo (MPM):** Thank you, Nicholas, for your interest in my writing and for inviting me for an interview. I am most definitely flattered—you had me at "truly great." I'm surprised to hear you feel it is a horror story. It does indeed have gruesome moments, but the rough predicaments and tortures depicted I based on treatments I've read about in journals and other historic documents.

It's also a study of humans and their seemingly bottomless ability to treat each other, nature, and animals with disdain and savagery. Therefore, I don't see *The Hunted* as a horrific novel, but as an exploration of various aspects of humanity and inhumanity. I hope that doesn't sound grandiose… Mostly I want to write ripping yarns with lots of action, romance, and danger.

As to what inspired *The Hunted*, as with all my books, its inspiration stems from a number of things—people I've met, places I've been, books I've read. It also has a healthy dose of some of my favorite subject matter, both as a reader and as a writer: cold, wintry settings. Whatever is challenging in wilting heat feels doubly difficult in extreme cold and blizzardlike conditions.

**LC:** It's a fairly long novel, and anyone who has read it can clearly see that every sentence is deftly written. I've heard you say that you write your novels from beginning to end before any edits. How long did it take you to write and edit this one? With a couple of successful

Ralph Compton novels under your belt already, was writing *The Hunted* a faster, smoother process than with the other two books?

**MPM:** Thanks, yes, *The Hunted* is standard-length, roughly 80,000 words. I do like to write novels from beginning to end, no looking back. It works for me, keeps it a fresher storytelling experience. Then I go back and rework it for as long as it needs. I wrote *The Hunted* in 2012 while working on other projects, and all in all, it took a few months.

Yes, overall the novel-writing process is becoming more familiar. I feel I'm getting better with each book at writing a cleaner first draft, though I still take as much time as I'm able to go over and over the manuscript.

**LC:** In keeping with all your Westerns, there are a good number of despicably savage characters in *The Hunted*. The Shoshoni Indian, Blue Dog Moon, is perhaps the most sadistic of all, but Rollie Meecher doesn't appear to have any redeeming qualities. Do you enjoy creating grotesque villains? What would you say are the things you enjoy most about writing novels? And is there a moment when you're writing the plot or the novel itself when you say, can I put the character through that or is it too much?

**MPM:** Oh, I don't know, I think ol' Rollie Meecher isn't such a bad bloke. He just had a hard time growing up. Nah, on second thought he's a hydrophobic beast who deserves two in the hat. Who doesn't enjoy reading and writing about characters with certain over-the-top qualities? One of the things I most enjoy about writing is creating interesting characters, then putting them in challenging situations that test their skills—or lack of them.

There have not been too many moments in writing a novel when I've said, "Nah, that'd be too over the top." More often than not I'll say, "How much more can I put this goober through?" And then I push that. Readers seem to like this and it keeps the story hopping. That said, I work to keep situations believable and (somewhat) plausible, as opposed to being outlandish for no reason.

**LC:** One of the things that make *The Hunted* such a notable book is the character Charlie Chilton, also known as Shotgun Charlie. There must be a dozen unpleasant characters in the novel, with a few of them really loathsome, but in the case of Charlie you've managed to produce a very memorable, larger-than-life hero. It's almost as if, after creating a villain as powerful as Blue Dog Moon, you needed to think up someone who would be a believable match for him. You describe him as built like a bear and, later, you actually have him fighting wolves with his bare hands. How did the character come about? Did you have someone or perhaps even a bear in mind when you imagined him?

**MPM:** I'm pleased to hear you like Shotgun Charlie. I did indeed want to create a larger-than-life fellow. Ol' Charlie's one of my favorite characters—a quiet-type ass-kicker with a heart of gold. I had a few folks in mind—fictional and real—when I came up with him. Hoss from "Bonanza" is one, my father, a big man—a dairy farmer—quiet, thoughtful, and kind, is another. I didn't intentionally set out to make Charlie the antithesis of Blue Dog Moon, but I find your observation interesting.

I also would like to point out that Hester and her sister, Delia, are two tough cookies who take lickings and dole out kickings with the best of them. It's very important to me that my female characters be as distinctive, rugged, and heroic as their male counterparts. After all, the Old West wasn't really populated with square-jawed men in white hats protecting simpering women!

**LC:** Hester and Delia are strong characters, as you say, and your novels do usually contain strong-minded women who are able to cope with the harsh situations you put them in. Characters like Jenna Winters in *Winters' War* and Emma Farraday in *Tucker's Reckoning* prove to be just as physically capable as Hester is in *The Hunted*, in that they are able to tackle the villains themselves. In fact, Emma Farraday, with her men's denims, broad-brimmed hat, and work boots, who rides a horse like a man, is perhaps the most resilient character in *Tucker's Reckoning*. Do you think that having

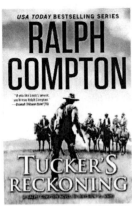

USA TODAY BESTSELLING SERIES
RALPH COMPTON

TUCKER'S RECKONING

Tucker's Reckoning
New American Library | 2012

a particularly strong female character like Emma as one of the two main characters in the book helped *Tucker's Reckoning* win the Spur Award? What would you say made that book your most endearing one? And what was your inspiration for Lord Tarleton, the English dandy? He seems rather different from your other characters.

**MPM:** I'm pleased you recognize the strong female characters in my books. I work hard to make sure they hold a bold, balanced place in my stories. I'm sure Emma Farraday has had a positive influence in helping make *Tucker's Reckoning* popular with readers, primarily because she's a tough, no-nonsense character who makes things happen.

As to inspiration for Lord Tarleton, I believe he is an amalgam of several characters and snippets of information I've read about or met or experienced. Back in the day, overprivileged travelers from a number of countries made their way to the American West, some with a yen to accumulate new experiences, some to gobble up resources and make bigger fortunes before moving on, leaving scars and wreckage in their wakes. Tarleton's definitely one of the latter, and so fun to write about.

**LC:** You said in an interview once: "I knew I was going to let someone escape from a fight, but at the last minute, he seemed to need to die." Of all your characters, the hardest one to see put in peril was the droll old-timer Squirly Ross, in *Dead Man's Ranch*. When you were writing that book, was there a moment when you considered sparing Squirly?

**MPM:** Squirly Ross is a special character who served his purpose and who had to lurch offstage, trailing blood and the shadows of a lifetime of good intentions. I rarely plan on peril-izing a character early on; rather, I find that situations arise in which I find that diminishing them will help heighten the drama and tighten the

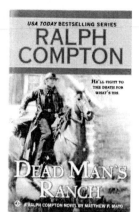

Dead Man's Ranch | Signet | 2012

tension. I try to not be too sentimental about my characters because then the story will be toothless and predictable and more closely resemble a church social event than a thrilling tale of adventure. That said, I do feel badly when I lay low a character I've come to enjoy spending time with, as I did with ol' Squirly.

LC: I've read that your first three novels were scheduled to be published by Leisure Books, an imprint of Dorchester Publishing, but the demise of Dorchester's mass-market paperback line persuaded you to withdraw from the publishing deal. The books were subsequently published by the great UK-based publisher Robert Hale Ltd, as part of their Black Horse Western series. As you were a first-time author and both of these were well-known publishing houses, was it a difficult process placing *Winters' War*, the first of these novels, with either publisher?

MPM: Well, you're slightly mistaken in the sequence of events. Those three books were first published by Robert Hale Ltd, as part of their Black Horse Western line. Then the offer from Dorchester came to reprint them as mass-market paperbacks for the US audience. Unfortunately, Dorchester imploded shortly thereafter. So my wife and I retooled the books, significantly in a number of ways, and reissued them as ebooks via our own imprint, Gritty Press (grittypress.com).

It wasn't particularly difficult to sell *Winters' War* to Hale for the BHW line. I read their guidelines, joined the Yahoo group for and run by writers for the line, and was given excellent advice by a number of those writers. Then I worked on the story some more until it felt right, sent it off, and was thrilled to receive the acceptance. Hale was a wonderful publisher to deal with, very attentive and responsive. I can't recommend them highly enough.

**LC:** Ever since 2007, you've had more than a dozen books published and your short stories have appeared in more than a dozen anthologies. Were you writing fiction prior to 2007? And how did you get involved with Moonstone Books and DAW Books, the latter being, primarily, a science fiction and fantasy publisher?

**MPM:** Actually, since 2007, I've had about two dozen books published, a number of them under "house names" for various lines. I believe about half of my books have been non-fiction, half of them novels.

I have written fiction for many years, and started publishing stories, poems, and articles back in high school. It wasn't until 2000 or so that I began getting serious about writing and submitting fiction. I didn't consider tackling a novel for a few years because it seemed like such a daunting task, but I finally took an online novel writing course that was useful.

I ended up getting my MFA degree in writing in 2003 and that proved tremendously helpful. My first novel, *Go Fish!*, a satirical comedic romp about pro bass fishing and America's over-commercialization, came out of that. A few early readers compared it to a Coen Brothers film. It is unpublished, but that might soon change. Stay tuned…

Regarding contributing to the Moonstone anthologies, I was fortunate to know Howard Hopkins, a top-notch and prolific writer of Westerns, horror, and young adult novels who, sadly, passed away not long ago. I encourage readers to read his work—it's great. He was also editing anthologies for Moonstone Books and offered me spots in a couple of them. I've edited a few anthologies myself, so I appreciate what a hefty task they can be.

With the stories I did for the DAW Books anthologies, it was a matter of having come to know the fine writer Jean Rabe through other avenues—I contributed to a newsletter she edited for International Association of Media Tie-In Writers (IAMTW). She had edited a number of anthologies and when new ones came up, she asked me if I might be interested in contributing. I wrote a time-travel Western story for *Timeshares* and for *Steampunk'd!* I wrote "Scourge of the Spoils." That story ended up nominated for a Western Fictioneers Peacemaker Award. Since then I've worked up plans for a series of books based on the story. The first novel is written and I'm currently editing it.

**LC:** In the past you've said, "With fiction, I prefer to keep mum about work that's not published yet, unless it's about to be." This sounds like a good indicator that *Go Fish!* has found a publisher already. Is that the case? Incidentally, I know you've contributed articles to fishing magazines in the past. I take it you're a fishing aficionado?

**MPM:** That may well be the case—mum's the word.

And as far as fishing goes, I'm no aficionado, just someone who enjoys wetting a line now and again. Fly-fishing is a pleasant pastime that allows folks to get out and about in the great outdoors, away from the gadgets and gewgaws that we have all made part of our daily lives (cell phones, computers, etc.). I've never cared if I caught any fish, merely "standing in a river, waving a stick" (to paraphrase the excellent essayist, John Gierach) is a relaxing, contemplative way to spend time. I've also had the good fortune to work in an editorial capacity on a couple of fishing magazines.

**LC:** You've said that you write what interests you, and you've also said that, as a kid, you wanted to see your name on a mass-market paperback. Did you always want to write genre fiction? Am I correct in thinking that, so far, all your published novels have been Westerns? What made you decide to focus chiefly on writing fiction in the Western field?

**MPM:** I always wanted to write fun, ripping tales that made me howl with delight when I wrote them and made readers howl (hopefully not in pain!) when they read them. Because that's the sort of reading material I have always enjoyed. Growing up, I never considered what genre a book might be from, I wanted to read a good story. Distinctions such as "genre" versus "literary" generally create divisions that aren't useful, at least to me as a writer and as a reader. I read what interests me, and I do the same with writing.

So far my published novels have been set in the American West, but the coming year should see a change in that mix. I choose Westerns because I love reading them and writing about the region, the time period, and the characters who populate it. I also choose to work in the "Western" genre because there was and is room in the market. And, for that, I feel fortunate.

**LC:** I read that you write somewhere between 20,000 to 30,000 words per week. Am I correct in thinking that you have a number of other completed manuscripts awaiting publication? Some of the projects I've read about include a contemporary comic adventure series, a noir crime novel, and a second Roamer novel. You're also contributing a short novel to the Western Fictioneers' *West of the Big River* series. Can you talk about any of these books or are they still very much works in progress?

**MPH:** I only write lots of words in a week when I'm on deadline. Unfortunately, I'm on deadline much of the time these days. But it's great training and a fun experience. And when I get to feeling whiny about it, I remember all those jobs I've had that were less than ideal (though they did provide grist for the writing mill). I have a few other novels and novellas written, but not yet published. Some of them aren't ready, some of them hopefully are.

As I mentioned previously, this year will see new work out there, some Western-based, some non-Western. I prefer to keep mum about most of it until I have solid traction, but I can say the second Roamer novel (*Roamer, Book 2: The Greenhorn Gamble*) is in good shape. In fact, the first chapter is included as a teaser/bonus chapter at the end of the Gritty Press ebook of my novel, *Hot Lead, Cold Heart*.

**LC:** Among your short stories are adventures involving the characters Sherlock Holmes and the Avenger, Richard Henry Benson. Was it challenging writing tales involving these well-established characters, and are there any other literary characters you would love to write a short story about?

**MPM:** It was a bit challenging writing about established, well-known, and well-liked characters, but the fun factor overrode any difficulties that arose in the writing process. I believe readers liked my offerings. I enjoyed writing about those characters, their inherent quirks, and was fortunate enough in my Holmes story to include Arsene Lupin, the gentleman thief, who was a literary contemporary of Holmes. I very much enjoyed writing those stories for Moonstone Books and would love to contribute to future anthologies, should the opportunity arise.

Thank you, Nicholas, for this fun, wide-ranging interview. I'm flattered that you like my work and I hope to continue writing stories that readers like.

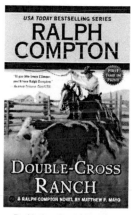

Double-Cross Ranch | Signet | 2014

*At the end of October, Matthew P. Mayo wrapped up his next Ralph Compton novel,* Double-Cross Ranch, *which will be published April 1st 2014. The novel is available to preorder from Amazon and elsewhere.*

# ROADSIDE ATTRACTION
**Matthew P. Mayo**

"Heck, in Africa, or some other foreign place, they call it bush meat."

"I don't care what they do in Africa. In America, they call that murder!"

Orrie squinted for a few quiet moments at Ruby, his 'assistant.' He should have known it would come to this, taking a dame on the circuit. An assistant with a heart. Jumpin' Jiminy on a pogo stick.... "You really are a softy, aren't you, Rube?"

"Go to hell."

He snorted and turned away.

Ruby plucked a fresh match from the book, raked it too hard. It didn't light.

"You'd rather starve to death than cut our losses and fill our bellies, huh?" said Orrie.

"Yeah, yeah I would, Orrie!" The bent cigarette bounced between her lips like a conductor's baton.

He hated that. Quick as an eye-blink, he clapped a palm hard against the side of the cage. A harsh clang echoed in the cramped, smelly tow trailer. "Well, not me, babe! I got needs—and places to be."

The bars were 3/4-inch steel rod, the angle-iron corners double-seamed and bolted tight. The massive, groggy creature in the cage, a hunched pile of thin brown hair, barely responded to Orrie's repeated banging on the cage. But it did fart and raise one eyelid.

"It's not like he can help it, Orrie. It ain't natural...." She waved a hand toward the cage as if she were drying her nails.

"Eatin' ain't a natural enough act for you?"

"That's not what I meant, Orrie, and you know it. That cage, the show. He's a wild creature, not some attraction."

Orrie pushed his boater far back on his head and blew out a long sigh. He kept his eyes closed as he spoke. "If this don't beat all. We're countin' our ribs here, the hairy wonder's gettin' a free ride, and you're worried about upsetting the natural balances of nature." He wondered what he ever did to be stuck like this with a mooching broad and a mooching bigfoot.

If I could turn back the clock, he thought, I would have folded in that game, not won the damn man-ape. Thing had brought him nothing but piss-poor luck for a couple of years now. He didn't have him a month when GoiterBoy and the Rattlesnake Woman up and got hitched, headed off to Arizona to live on a cactus ranch or something. That left him with Inky the Full-Color Man. Turned out the tattoos he'd been giving himself were full of lead, so he up and died. And since Inky had no relatives, Orrie had to shell out for the funeral.

Then he was down to just the hairball, a seven foot, 400-pound goober who couldn't talk, smelled like roadkill and stale sweat, and wouldn't act like a savage for the kiddies no matter how hard you poked him with a sharp stick.

Then one day, Orrie was up to his knees in man-ape shit, hoeing out the trailer, when Ruby showed up. Didn't seem to mind that he smelled like a hatful of rotten ass. Plus, she had an okay can and an idea that maybe she could help him out somehow should he consider taking her with him on the road.

Should have seen that one coming, he thought. Any spare change he used to have for a little wine of an evening went straight for her ciggies and hairdo. And that man-ape's diet, thought Orrie. Don't get me started...

And then there was the powder he had to sprinkle on everything the brute ate, just to keep it from tearing the cage apart—when the crowds weren't looking, naturally. That had happened exactly once before he wizened up, found a veterinarian who prescribed the bluish stuff. Said it was for use on zoo animals like elephants. Orrie believed it. Tried a lick himself and slept for two days. Missed a show, lost his gig, the works. Yessir, life had been a challenge since the hairy wonder had come along.

Truth was, Orrie had been lonely since Inky died. No one to talk to. He'd taken to sitting in the trailer at night, drinking spodee-o-dee special and talking to the bigfoot. But it just snored and grunted and farted like an old plow horse. Feeding the thing was killing his wallet. Still, somehow Orrie just knew that the beast was special like no other side-show attraction pounding the circuit. If only he could figure out how to get the money folks to take a gander. So far, though, they'd all stayed away.

But he kept thinking maybe he'd get a break, rent him out to the movies—now that's where the money was. But California was a long ways from the southeast circuit, and Orrie never seemed to have enough scratch to make the trip out there.

And here I am, he thought, driving through Pisspot, Tennessee, once again. Subbed myself out to a shit-rate traveling show, worst one on the circuit and my very last opportunity.

He was down to a couple of nickels that weren't multiplying, fumes in the tank, a flat on the left front, bald runners on the rest, no food in the backseat, a dame with feelings, and a well-fed manape getting chauffeured around in the trailer. Now, what can you do with that magic combination, Orrie? He'd asked himself that question just the night before, listening to Ruby snore like a drunk stevedore beside him.

He'd snitched one of her smokes and lay awake, blowing plumes at the stars, thinking of a good shank of beef, something for the stewpot, chopped steak, hell anything he could chew. His stomach had growled then, long and low, and he knew what he had to do.

\*

"We're just lucky the big bastard's still docile. I ain't told you yet, but I had to cut back on his damn fruits and berries. I even had to cut back on his powder doses. This batch runs out, I don't know what we'll do."

"Oh no, Orrie, it's not his fault."

He thumbed his temples. "All right already, heh? I got enough worries. Like how do I get the flat fixed so we can make it to the next gig. We don't get to the fairgrounds by four, we might as well keep going, 'cause that schmo Ryker told me he ain't in the mood for excuses."

Ruby stared at the cage, at the massive hunched form within. "Let him go." She looked at Orrie, grabbed his sleeve. "Oh please, Orrie, just set him free."

He had to hand it to her, what she said was pure Ruby. He shouldn't have laughed, but he did. "What? And watch his well-fed ass waddle off to live in the woods, without a care in the world? No siree, Bob, I aim to collect on my investment."

"I don't know what to say, Orrie." Ruby began to cry.

Orrie didn't fall for it, wouldn't let himself this time. He was too hungry—and too tired of this happy horseshit. "I'll tell you what to say, Rube. Say you'll help me put him out of his misery."

She pulled in a big swallow of air like it was on sale, her eyes dripping.

He ignored it and leaned against the cage. "Yep, I got it all figured out. I finally know how we're going to fill our bellies and make our mint." He looked at her, his eyes wide. "We'll skin him, Rube! Skin him out, cook him up, and save the hide. People do that sort of thing all the time. Like them hunters with their deers and ducks and whatnot. No problem. Then we get him stuffed, tote him around a while, won't have to feed him, shovel his shit, the works. And then we drive him—ready for this?" He lit a match for her; the flame flared up, danced in his shining eyes.

She snuffled and nodded, leaned next to him, drew on the cigarette.

"All the way to Hollywood, baby!" Orrie raised an arm as if he'd won a round of bingo. His shout turned into a short, strangled scream as his arm whipped backward, followed by his head, which disappeared straight back between two cage bars, slick as if it were greased. His straw hat pinwheeled into the shadows as a series of sounds, like carrots snapping, filled the air in the tiny trailer.

Just as she began to scream, the same thing happened to Ruby. *Pop-pop-pop.* One clip-on earring rolled across the floor. Ruby leaned limp, half-in, half-out of the cage, right next to Orrie, her smoking cigarette gripped tight in her teeth.

*

It had been years since he'd had fresh meat. All because he'd spent a little too long in that patch of fermented berries and fell asleep. Next thing he knew he'd been captured, sold, traded, lost and won in a card game, and then dragged all over creation by these bossy little hairless beasts.

He felt like he'd been half asleep through most of it, but heck if he wasn't feeling better by the minute. Get a little more of this meat inside of him, he'd pull these bars apart and head on up the road. Thinking he might try that 'Hollywood' place. The jackass had talked about it long enough, it was starting to sound pretty good.

Say what he would about the guy, if nothing else, Orrie was persuasive. And tasty.

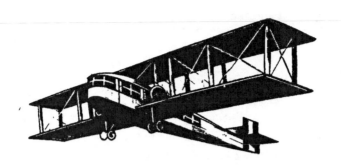

# CONTRIBUTORS

Nicholas Litchfield is the founding editor of *Lowestoft Chronicle* and author of the novel *Swampjack Virus*. Born in Britain, he has worked in numerous countries as a librarian, journalist, and researcher. He lives in Western New York.

Susan Moorhead's fiction and poetry has appeared in a variety of online and print journals, magazines, and anthologies. Recent work is in *Lowestoft Chronicle*, *Open to Interpretation: Intimate Landscape*, *Danse Macabre*, *Otis Nebula*, *Connecticut River Review*, and *Let the Poets Speak*.

Jason Braun currently teaches English and is the Associate Editor of *Sou'wester* at Southern Illinois University Edwardsville. He has published fiction, poetry, reported or been featured in *Prime Number*, ESPN.com, *The Evergreen Review*, SOFTBLOW, *The Nashville City Paper*, Jane Freidman's blog, *The Chronicle of Higher Education*, *Lowestoft Chronicle*, and many more. He also makes apps such as Paradise Lost Office and Homophonecheck.com, and releases music as Jason and the Beast.

John Dennehy grew up in New York, but moved out of the country when Bush was re-elected. For five years he lived in the developing world, mostly in Latin America, and returned to the United States in 2010. He is writing a book titled *Illegal* about his deportation from Ecuador during a nationalist revolution and works at the press office of the United Nations.

James Reasoner has been a professional writer for over thirty-five years. A Spur Award nominee and Peacemaker winner, his books have appeared on the *New York Times* and *USA Today* bestseller lists. He lives in a small town in Texas with his wife, award-winning fellow author Livia J. Washburn.

Rob McClure Smith's fiction has appeared in *Barrelhouse*, *Fugue*, *Manchester Review*, *Lowestoft Chronicle*, and many other literary magazines.

Andrew House works as a writing tutor in Muncie, Indiana, where he is pursuing a degree in creative writing. He balances his creative efforts between horror fiction and humorous poetry.

Sue Granzella fell in love with writing at age six, but until two years ago she mostly wrote fiery union emails and speeches to her school board. She started taking writing classes after meeting an artist in Massachusetts who inspired her to give in to her passion. She has won five awards for her work, including first place in the Soul-Making Keats Literary Competition. Her work appears in *Prick of the Spindle*, *Switchback*, *Rougarou*, *Apeiron Review*, and *Lowestoft Chronicle*. She teaches third grade in Hayward, loves baseball, stand-up comedy, hiking, and reading the writing of 8-and 9-year-olds.

Chuck Redman has practiced law in Los Angeles for 35 years. His novella *The Meateaters* was published serially in *Between the Species* (1986-87). More recently, his short fiction has appeared in *Lowestoft Chronicle*, *Writer's Digest*, *Hemlock Journal*, and *The Jewish Magazine*.

Jay Parini is a distinguished poet, novelist, biographer and critic. His books of poetry include *The Art of Subtraction: New and Selected Poems*, and he has written volumes of essays and critical studies, as well as biographies of John Steinbeck, Robert Frost, and William Faulkner. His novels include *Benjamin's Crossing*, *The Apprentice Lover*, *The Passages of H.M.*, and *The Last Station*, which was turned into an Academy Award-nominated film starring Helen Mirren, Christopher Plummer, and Paul Giamatti.

Michael Solomon is a documentary filmmaker and the author of the 2012 memoir *Now It's Funny: How I Survived Cancer, Divorce and Other Looming Disasters* (www.nowitsfunny.com). His blog appears on *The Huffington Post*.

Jackie Strawbridge received her BA in English and French from Boston University. She currently lives in Paris.

Yvonne Pesquera has a bachelor's degree in creative writing from New York University. She presently workshops her fiction at Grub Street, the esteemed Boston writers' school, and has attended a weeklong fiction intensive at the Harvard University Extension School. Her short story, "Pits from the Cherry Tree," was selected from hundreds of submissions and published in the *Harvard Summer Review 2010*.

Michael C. Keith is the author of two-dozen books on media, a young adult novel, five short story collections, and the acclaimed memoir, *The Next Better Place*. He also co-edited a found manuscript by legendary writer/director Norman Corwin. He has been nominated for the Pushcart Prize and PEN/O.Henry Award and is the recipient of numerous awards in his academic field. He teaches communication at Boston College. His website address is www.michaelckeith.com.

George Moore's *The Hermits of Dingle* was released last summer by FutureCycle Press. His fifth collection, *Children's Drawings of the Universe*, will be published by Salmon Poetry Press in 2014. Moore's poetry has appeared in *The Atlantic*, *Poetry*, *North American Review*, *Colorado Review*, *Lowestoft Chronicle*, and he has been a finalist for a number of book awards, including The National Poetry Series. He lives with his wife, the Canadian poet, Tammy Armstrong, in Colorado and Nova Scotia.

Ed Hamilton is the author of *Legends of the Chelsea Hotel: Living with the Artists and Outlaws of New York's Rebel Mecca* (Da Capo, 2007). His fiction has appeared in various journals, including: *Limestone Journal*, *The Journal of Kentucky Studies*, *River Walk Journal*, *Exquisite Corpse*, *Modern Drunkard Magazine*, *Lumpen*, and, most recently, in *Lowestoft Chronicle*, *Omphalos*, *Bohemia*, *Penduline*, and in the anthology, *Poetic Story*. His fiction has also appeared in translation in Czechoslovakia's *Host*.

Kim Farleigh has worked for aid agencies in three conflicts: Kosovo, Iraq, and Palestine. He takes risks to get the experience required for writing. He likes fine wine, art, photography, and bullfighting, which probably explains why this Australian lives in Madrid.

Nancy Caronia is a Ph.D. candidate in English Literature at the University of Rhode Island. Her creative work has been anthologized in *The Milk of Almonds: Italian American Women Writers on Food and Culture, Don't Tell Mama! The Penguin Book of Italian American Writing*, and *Coloring Book: An Eclectic Anthology of Multicultural Writers*. She and Edvige Giunta have a forthcoming co-edited collection: *Personal Effects: Essays on Culture, Teaching, and Memoir in the Work of Louise DeSalvo*.

Thomas Piekarski is a former editor of the *California State Poetry Quarterly*. His theater and restaurant reviews have been published in various newspapers, with poetry and interviews appearing in numerous national journals, among them *Portland Review, Main Street Rag, Kestrel, Scarlet Literary Magazine, Cream City Review, Nimrod, Penny Ante Feud, New Plains Review, Poetry Quarterly, The Muse-an International Journal of Poetry*, and *Clockhouse Review*. He has published a travel guide, *Best Choices In Northern California*, and *Time Lines*, a book of poems. He lives in Marina, California.

Tim Conley's fiction, poetry, essays, and translations have appeared in journals from a variety of different countries. He is currently completing his third collection of short fiction.

Laine Strutton is an interdisciplinary PhD Candidate at New York University. She is currently writing her dissertation on women's oil protests in Nigeria. She has pieced together every form of alternative travel she could on a student's budget, including work in Korea, Mozambique, Kyrgyzstan, Honduras, and Bolivia.

Nick LaRocca is Associate Professor of English at Palm Beach State College. He lives in Delray Beach, Florida, with his wonderful wife and two dogs. He has published short stories and essays most recently in *Lowestoft Chronicle*, *Steel Toe Review*, *Rush Hour: Bad Boys* (Delacorte Press), and *Mason's Road*, and is the recipient of the Robert Wright Prize for Writing Excellence.

Matthew P. Mayo has written more than twenty-five books and dozens of short stories. His novel, *Tucker's Reckoning*, won the Western Writers of America's 2013 Spur Award for Best Western Novel. He has also been a Spur finalist in the Short Fiction category and a Western Fictioneers Peacemaker Award finalist. His novels include *Winters' War*; *Wrong Town*; *Hot Lead, Cold Heart*; *Dead Man's Ranch*; *Tucker's Reckoning*; *The Hunted*; *Double-Cross Ranch*; and many more. He also contributes to other popular series of Western and adventure novels. His nonfiction books include *Cowboys, Mountain Men & Grizzly Bears*; *Bootleggers, Lobstermen & Lumberjacks*; *Sourdoughs, Claim Jumpers & Dry Gulchers*; *Haunted Old West*; *Speaking Ill of the Dead: Jerks in New England History*, and numerous others. He collaborated with his wife, photographer Jennifer Smith-Mayo, on a series of popular hardcover books, including *Maine Icons*, *New Hampshire Icons*, and *Vermont Icons*. The Mayos also run Gritty Press (www.GrittyPress.com) and rove North America in their Airstream trailer in search of hot coffee, tasty whiskey, and high adventure. Stop by Matthew's website (www.MatthewMayo.com) for a chin-wag and a cuppa mud.

# COPYRIGHT NOTES

# ACKNOWLEDGEMENTS

With special thanks to Amie McLaughlin for her priceless feedback and suggestions and for all the proofreading she has done for the magazine for the last two and a half years. Special thanks also to Tara for all her help and advice with the magazine and her outstanding design work, and to Matthew P. Mayo, Frank Mundo, James Reasoner, and Michael C. Keith. The magazine wouldn't exist if it weren't for the marvelous contributors we've been fortunate to publish. Much gratitude to everyone who has contributed to the magazine.

# Bon Voyage!

The popular literary magazine presents its first Best Of!

# Lowestoft Chronicle
# 2011 Anthology

### Edited by Nicholas Litchfield

The world has gone digital. The physical book has been replaced by an electronic one; the family vacation has been replaced by the 'work retreat'. Today, the print anthology seems as unfashionable and outdated as the notion of travel for recreational purposes. In defiance of social trends and common sense we bring you the *LOWESTOFT CHRONICLE 2011 ANTHOLOGY*—a collection of our favorite stories, poems, and creative non-fiction pieces from the first year of our quarterly online magazine.

Lose yourself in the work of Lisa Abellera, Jennine Capó Crucet, Tim Conley, Michael Connor, Ron D'Alena, Brinna Deavellar, William Doreski, Laury A. Egan, Jack Frey, Katherine Hinkebein, Tyke Johnson, Michael C. Keith, Tom Mahony, Eric G. Müller, Jeremy Rich, Frank Roger, Phil Smith III, Davide Trame, Howard Waldman, and Aida Zilelian.

### PRAISE FOR THE WORK IN
### LOWESTOFT CHRONICLE 2011 ANTHOLOGY

"This is a fine anthology that I found both provocative and enjoyable. Highest praise: it made me want to write short stories again."
—Luke Rhinehart, author of the cult classic *The Dice Man*

"Michael Connor's 'Stevie and Louie' is a fun read about a young, single tourist in Austin ... 'The Shooting Party' by Jack Frey is a story of a chance encounter in an exotic location that is both plausible and mysterious. It makes good use of dialogue and an inventive plot."
—*New York Journal of Books*

"Another good one is a tongue-in-cheek piece of fiction entitled 'The Last Election' by Frank Roger, about a group of men electing a pope as the planet around them is gradually being destroyed by earthquakes. It is quite possible the last man standing will become the de facto pope, but will have little opportunity to fulfill his papal ambitions."
—*Newpages.com*

"Poems such as Laury Egan's 'Point No Point' show a journal that chooses poetry with keen regard to the specificity and the ache of place."
—Barth Landor, author of *A Week in Winter*

**To order, visit www.lowestoftchronicle.com**

Another Best Of from the popular literary magazine!

# Far-flung and Foreign

## Edited by Nicholas Litchfield

Action, intrigue, romance and adventure—your boss may not be familiar with these words, and if he is he may not think they occur outside the workplace. This is your chance to tell him he's wrong. Beyond his wilting glare beckons the shimmering, fun-packed FAR-FLUNG AND FOREIGN.

Laden with dragons, lepers and Barbie dolls, and transporting readers to far-flung places, we proudly present the work of Vanessa Blakeslee, Will Buckingham, Joan L. Cannon, Lorraine Caputo, Martina Clark, Rijn Collins, Laury A. Egan, Michael Frissore, Bruce Gatenby, Kathie Giorgio, Charles Haddox, Rick Hartwell, Paul Kavanagh, Michael C. Keith, Benjamin Kensey, Wayne Lee, A. L. Means, Nicholas Rombes, Gordon West, and Scott Younkin. Also includes an exclusive interview with comic book writer Augustine Funnell.

Whether bronzing on the company yacht, dipping strawberries in a glass of warm champagne, or at the ski lodge, reclining on the bearskin rug by an open fire with your drink of choice and man or woman of the hour, this collection is something you can fondle lovingly whatever the season.

### PRAISE FOR THE WORK IN FAR-FLUNG AND FOREIGN

"Hot off the press, and fresh from the mail, [is] this terrific anthology culled from *Lowestoft Chronicle* from 2011. The writing here is fresh, surprising, and alive. Not to be missed is the bittersweet interview with the author Augustine Funnell. (Please write more!) The book looks and feels great."
— Nicholas Rombes, acclaimed author of
*A Cultural Dictionary of Punk: 1974-1982*

"I immensely enjoyed 'The Adventures of Root Beer Float Man' by Michael Frissore. For poetry, try Wayne Lee's 'Ordinary Deckhand.'"
— *Newpages.com*

'I've enjoyed reading the *Chronicle*. 'I Like Your Deer's Moustache, and other Lithuanian Tales'...[is] a distinctly Baltic twist on mistaken identity. One of our most popular pieces."
— *My Audio Universe*
(Rijn Collin's story aired on the independent radio station KVMR).

To order, visit www.lowestoftchronicle.com

The acclaimed literary magazine presents its third Best Of!

# Intrepid Travelers

## Edited by Nicholas Litchfield

Featuring the work of Jada Ach, Jack Austin, Brian Conlon, Steve Gronert Ellerhoff, Bruce Gatenby, Sharleen Jonsson, Michael C. Keith, David Klein, Hector S. Koburn, Barth Landor, Robert Mangeot, dl mattila, Mark J. Mitchell, Lynn E. Palermo, Tamara Kaye Sellman, Denise Thompson-Slaughter, and Dennis Vanvick. Also includes exclusive interviews with foremost David Dodge biographer Randal S. Brandt, legendary Western writer James Reasoner, and *New York Times* bestselling author and intrepid traveler Franz Wisner.

PRAISE FOR THE WORK IN INTREPID TRAVELERS

"Many short stories and poems here offer deeper meanings and address heavier topics. 'Something Like Culture Shock' by Dennis Vanvick…[has] good character development and a compelling story. 'Political Awakening, 1970' by Denise Thompson-Slaughter…it was refreshing to read a piece with this much depth. 'Pájaro Diablo' by Michael C. Keith…by the end, the reader is riveted to see what will happen next. Also features an interview with Randal S. Brandt… [which] has enough information and material to make for an entertaining read. Overall, this is full of great talent and exceptionally written pieces."
— *The Review Review*

"Refreshing and well-written, *Intrepid Travelers* takes the reader to a wide variety of literary destinations, and makes even a confirmed hermit like me want to get up and go somewhere. Highly recommended."
— James Reasoner, *Rough Edges*

"Prepare for an adrenalin surge as a thief tries to escape from armed Mafia agents in Hector S. Koburn's fatalistic 'Bloody Driving Gloves,' Steve Gronert Ellerhoff's brilliantly quirky short story, 'Apophallation,' [and] Michael C. Keith's unexpectedly moving 'Pájaro Diablo.' *Intrepid Travelers* is a coruscating cornucopia of humour, drama and big, beautiful adventures. Highly original and entertaining."
—Pam Norfolk, *Lancashire Evening Post*

"Contains a fascinating interview with Randal S. Brandt about his discovery of a lost manuscript by the author David Dodge…Excellent fiction, poetry, and non-fiction."
— Nicholas Rombes, author of *Ramones* and *New Punk Cinema*

"Without a single stinker or filler piece in the bunch. I was extremely impressed with the variety and quality of the writing. *Intrepid Travelers* is a solid collection of funny and fine travel-themed stories, poetry, essays and interviews that easily fits in a back pocket or carry-on bag."
— *Examiner.com*

To order, visit www.lowestoftchronicle.com

926

CPSIA information can be obtained at www.ICGtesting.com
Printed in the USA
LVOW08s0853270414

383421LV00001B/59/P

9 780982 536575